Shattered Calm

Happy Reading!
Susan Maroney

SUSAN MARONEY

Copyright © 2023 Susan Maroney
All rights reserved
First Edition

PAGE PUBLISHING
Conneaut Lake, PA

First originally published by Page Publishing 2023

ISBN 978-1-6624-8447-6 (pbk)
ISBN 978-1-6624-8448-3 (digital)

Printed in the United States of America

CHAPTER 1

Unseemly Deeds

"Sarah, do you have a few minutes?" asked Ralph Benson. "I must speak with you."

"Certainly, Ralph. What is it?" replied Sarah.

"Last night I received a call. I have no idea who it was. I am not even sure whether it was a male or female, the voice was so disguised. Whoever it was warned me that my custodial job here at the Women's Club is in jeopardy, and before hanging up, shouted obscenities. After I hung up, I was really upset. I kept hearing the words over and over in my head and could not get to sleep. I don't know what to do."

Sarah was taken aback. She was not sure what to say, but she wanted to calm Ralph's nerves.

"Ralph, for the time being, let's just consider it a prank call. Try not to worry about it, but please let me know immediately if it happens again, and we will notify the police."

"Thanks, Sarah, for listening to me and for your support. Thinking that it was just a prank call does make me feel somewhat better. Hopefully, there will be no repeat episodes."

"I hope not too," said Sarah. "If I can be of any further help, I'll be here for several hours."

"Thank you," replied Ralph.

Sarah Peterson, a petite, strikingly pretty woman in her forties with shoulder-length auburn hair, deep brown eyes, and a rosy complexion was president of the Calm Woods Cove Women's Club. The Women's Club's clubhouse was the scene of many social gatherings, educational programs, cultural events, and meetings. A variety of club departments sponsored monthly speakers across a broad range of topics, and throughout the year, there were luncheons, parties of all types, book discussions, and day trips to New York City.

The Women's Club sponsored several major fundraisers each year. Funds from these events supported the charitable gifts the club provided to local organizations. The funds were also used to maintain the historic clubhouse, a charming Dutch colonial building built in the 1930s in the center of town.

The Women's Club has been closely associated with almost every aspect of life in Calm Woods Cove. The club prided itself on responding to the needs of the community and beyond. Community service projects over the years have been large and small, but there was hardly a local charity or town organization that has not benefited from the club's presence. Every year, the club donated thousands of dollars to local charities, especially focusing on those that helped women and children.

Sarah has been a member of the Women's Club for ten years. She joined the club with the hope of making new friends and participating in activities that would have an impact on the community. Both goals have been achieved. Sarah has met many women through the Women's Club, and most of her close friends were members of the club. She has also either chaired or served on committees that have reached out to help with the needs of the community. Over the years, Sarah has served on the Board of Directors of the Women's Club in numerous capacities. At present, she was just finishing her first year of a two-year term as president. She was well-liked by club members and was extremely dedicated to fulfilling the duties of her position.

After speaking with Ralph, Sarah spent the day presiding over a board meeting and then working through a pile of mail and answering a dozen phone messages. Sarah loved being president of the

Women's Club, but as the day wore on, she felt an ominous cloud hanging over her. She was being haunted by what Ralph Benson had told her that morning. She had responded that it probably was just a prank call, but now she was not so sure.

John Stephenson who had been a custodian at the Women's Club for twenty years had died from a massive coronary four months ago. The Women's Club struggled for a month to find his replacement. Eight men had submitted their resumes, and four were chosen to be interviewed. After much soul-searching, Ralph Benson was hired. It was determined that he possessed the high level of competency, specialized skills, and cheerful personality needed for the job. He was quite pleased to be chosen since the position came with a good salary, generous benefits, and lots of prestige.

A nagging question now kept running through Sarah's mind, *Was someone trying to take those things away from Ralph?*

Finally, Sarah was ready to go home, but before leaving the clubhouse, she decided to check in with Ralph. She found him busily cleaning the kitchen.

"How are you doing, Ralph?" asked Sarah.

"Okay. I just hope I don't get another call."

"Let me know immediately if you do."

"I will."

"I am leaving for home now unless you need me for something."

"No, all is well. Have a good evening."

"Thanks. You, too."

Sarah's drive home took less than ten minutes, and she fretted about Ralph's call the whole time.

It had to have been a prank, she repeated numerous times to herself, hoping that by repeating it enough times, it would turn out to be true.

Calm Woods Cove had a special reputation as being a friendly and welcoming place to live. It was a picturesque town, rich in history, culture, education, and natural beauty, with distinctive homes on quiet tree-lined streets. But most importantly, it had an almost nonexistent crime rate. It was said that you could live, work, and play there feeling completely safe. Now Sarah was beginning to wonder about this claim.

Sarah turned into her driveway, opened the garage, and pulled into it. Before she could spend any more time obsessing over Ralph's phone call, she was distracted by the welcoming barking of Bella, the family puppy. As she opened the door from the garage into the kitchen area, Bella jumped up to exchange "hello" greetings with her.

Bella had come to live with the Petersons three years ago when one of their neighbors was suddenly transferred to China and was not able to take Bella, a twelve-pound white Bichon Poo, along with him. Being absolutely adorable to look at, with her almond-shaped eyes, moderately long ears, and a short round muzzle, she immediately became a beloved member of the Peterson family. Sarah called Bella her "white fluff bundle of cheer" because she was intelligent, gentle-mannered, good-natured, playful, and had lots of energy to burn. Bella loved company, so she demanded attention and affection and was a wonderful cuddly companion.

After having a quick glass of juice, Sarah decided that since it was such a beautiful day, both she and Bella needed to take a walk. She found Bella's leash and then the two proceeded outside. Sarah loved walking around her neighborhood. All her neighbors' properties were beautifully landscaped, and the sights and scents were amazing. Sarah could feel herself gradually relaxing as she took in all the new spring blossoms—lilac and deep purple rhododendrons, bright pink and red azaleas, blue and white hydrangeas, bright yellow forsythia bushes, and on and on.

After about forty minutes of walking, Sarah reluctantly decided she had better return home to fix dinner. Once inside, after taking off Bella's leash, Sarah refilled Bella's water bowl and then proceeded to make dinner. She made pasta primavera, a large Caesar salad, and prepared a loaf of Italian bread with garlic butter to be put in the oven just before it was time to sit down for dinner. Next, she went to the breakfast room to set the dining table. She placed an arrangement of hydrangeas from her garden in the middle of it, and since the table overlooked the backyard garden and patio, Sarah shot a glance outside. She was surprised by a family of deer looking back at her, and then suddenly stopped and began eating the hostas she had recently planted. This did not make her happy, but she had to smile because the deer seemed so content. After about five minutes, they ran off and Sarah resumed setting the table.

At 6:00 p.m., Bob arrived home. Bob Peterson has been happily married to Sarah, whom he considered his soulmate, for some twenty-seven years. Bob was a handsome man who looked much younger than his fifty years of age. He was six feet tall and had brown hair with only a slight greying at the temples, and was in great shape thanks to his love of jogging. As CEO of a top pharmaceutical firm, Bob has been a wonderful provider for his family.

Bob kissed Sarah hello and then looked at her admiringly. *She is still as beautiful as the day I met her*, he thought.

Sarah then interrupted his complimentary thoughts. "Bob, I want your opinion on something that Ralph Benson told me today. Last night he received a call threatening his custodial job. Needless to say, he was very upset and wanted to see my reaction to the call. Before I tell you what I said, tell me your thoughts."

"I think it was a prank call, exceedingly cruel, but nothing more than a prank, However, if Ralph gets another one, then we have to contact the police," said Bob.

"That is pretty much what I said. I feel better that you agree with what I told him."

Sarah sighed and then said, "Now we can have dinner."

Sarah and Bob had a delightfully relaxing meal, even Bella joined them. Sarah had put a bowl of dog food near the table, and she and Bob were highly amused by the sound of Bella enthusiastically crunching her food. And while Sarah and Bob enjoyed chocolate ice cream for dessert, Bella chomped away on several doggie treats which she appeared to find delicious.

After dinner, Bob went off to take care of some work items, and Sarah cleaned up the kitchen. While doing so, she kept looking out the window over her sink in hopes of again seeing the deer, but they were nowhere in sight. After she finished cleaning up, she thought to herself, *I think I will go see what damage the deer did.*

But before she got to this, it suddenly hit her. *I forgot to fill out the forms for the upcoming Club 50/50 raffle. As much as I don't want to, I better go back to the clubhouse now.*

Sarah ran a comb through her hair, grabbed her coat and briefcase, and went to find her husband.

"Bob, I have to run to the clubhouse and take care of something I forgot to do today. I'll be back in an hour."

"Can't you wait until tomorrow? I don't like you going there alone at night. I'd go with you but I'm expecting a call from Indianapolis."

"I really want to get it done while I'm thinking about it. It has to do with the 50/50 raffle the club is having at the annual meeting. The proceeds will provide camp scholarships for needy children. It is such a good cause, so I want to make sure I get all the needed filings done with more than enough time to spare."

"Okay, but be sure you lock the doors and turn on lots of lights."

"Don't worry, I'll be fine. See you soon."

Sarah hurried out the door and into her car. The drive to the clubhouse took only seven minutes. She pulled into the parking lot. Except for a light shining from a flood lamp high up in a tree, all was pitch black. Sarah wanted to turn around and go home. She hated going to the clubhouse alone at night. She was always afraid someone would jump out at her in the parking lot. And once inside, she was always on edge because she heard disturbing sounds coming from the large gracious rooms. She believed it was just the old heating pipes doing their jobs, but it was unnerving.

Finally, she encouraged herself to get moving and parked by the back door. As she got out of her car, the newly installed motion-activated security light came on illuminating the entrance. She fumbled for a key and unlocked the door. She entered the kitchen and reached to flip on the kitchen light and turned to lock the door. She then let out a gasp.

The kitchen was filled with boxes of china, silverware, and glassware for an upcoming rental event. Sarah did not know how she was going to get around them, but she finally worked out a path and reached the entrance to the long hallway leading to the first-floor office. She tried to reach the light switch to turn on the chandeliers in the hallway, but she was hindered by even more boxes of deliveries.

Just great, she thought. *I should have brought a flashlight. I'm sure there is one in the kitchen, but heaven knows where.*

Sarah looked down the hall toward the office to see if she could find her way in the gloom. It was very dark except for a green glowing sign and two red security lights. It was cold too. The furnace was turned way down for the night. Sarah shivered.

If I keep a straight path down the middle, I should be okay, she thought. *I just hope all the furniture is where it belongs.*

Her footsteps echoed on the brick floor. Suddenly she slipped. She reached out and touched a chair which kept her from falling. She took a deep breath and fought the urge to run home. Instead, she resumed walking. Near the end of the hall, she quickened her pace and reached the office door. She unlocked and opened it and switched on the lights.

It is spooky in here, but at least it's quiet. I'll be able to get my work done quickly with no distractions.

Sarah turned on the computer, and while waiting for it to load the program she needed, she looked out the window facing the street. In contrast to the heavy daytime traffic, only an occasional car passed by. The computer was ready. Sarah found the forms she needed and began filling them out. Her fingers raced across the keyboard.

Almost done. I hope the letter I need to go with this is in my mailbox.

She walked to a series of boxes set into the wall. Each officer of the club had her own slot. Sarah tiptoed over to hers. Just as she reached for the contents, she heard a strange sound. Her heart almost leapt to her throat.

"Hello? Is anyone there?" Sarah called out.

All was quiet.

Maybe it was an animal outside or a branch hitting the building, she rationalized. She grabbed the letter and returned to the computer. She sat down and began perusing it to make sure she had done everything correctly on the form. Once she was convinced everything was in order, she clicked Print. While waiting for her copy, she thought she heard something again—sounded like footsteps.

Bob has made my imagination more fertile than usual with his comments, she thought. *I must admit I'll be glad to get out of here.*

Just at that moment, a loud noise rang out. The mirror on the wall behind the computer shattered and fell. Sarah sat frozen in her seat—unable to move—wondering what was going to happen next. She listened carefully for several minutes, but she heard nothing. She finally decided that she would watch the clock in front of her, and if she was still alive after ten minutes, she would get up, crossover to the desk, grab the phone, and call 911.

She spent ten minutes watching the clock and praying. Finally, the time was up, and she ran to the phone and dialed 911. Near tears, Sarah identified herself and explained what had happened and then said, "Please help me."

"Mrs. Peterson, just stay calm. If there is a desk in the room, crawl under it and wait for us. We are on our way."

Within a few minutes, three squad cars carrying six officers arrived at the clubhouse. One of the officers comforted Sarah and led her out of the office to a chair in the hallway. Once settled there, the officer questioned Sarah and took down her statement. The next two officers were assigned to inspecting the office crime scene, while the rest searched the building. After fifteen minutes, everyone met in the hallway outside the office door. They reported that they had found nothing—nothing except a bullet in the wall behind the shattered mirror. Nothing else seemed to be astray.

Suddenly, there was a loud knock at the back door. An officer ran to the kitchen and returned with Bob, to whom he had explained what happened.

"Sarah, are you all right?" asked Bob. "I was worried because you had been gone so long. I decided to come down to check on you and keep you company. Words cannot express what I felt when I saw the police cars here."

"Bob, I am fine. Rather shaken, but fine. I just can't understand what happened here tonight. Why would anyone shoot a mirror in the office of the Women's Club?"

"Mrs. Peterson," an officer interrupted, "I believe we have all the basic information, unless you have thought of something we should know?"

"No, nothing else comes to mind, but is it possible for you to get me the form that I had just printed and to turn off the printer?"

The officer returned with the form and also Sarah's purse.

"Thank you so much," Sarah said.

"You are most welcome," replied the officer and added, "Now you and your husband should go home and get some rest. We are going to do a thorough search again of the building and then keep watch overnight. We would appreciate it if you would go down to police headquarters in the morning to file a formal report."

CHAPTER 2

Club Day

Sarah and Bob walked into the Calm Woods Cove Police station promptly at nine the next morning. They were greeted by Captain David Blanchard, a good friend of theirs dating back some twenty years.

"Sarah and Bob, come with me. I want to introduce you to Detective Jack Smith whom I'm assigning to your case. He is one of my best men."

After passing a number of desks, they arrived at the door of Detective Smith's office. Captain Blanchard knocked.

"Come in," was the reply.

They went inside the office, and Captain Blanchard made the introductions. A tall, good-looking man in his forties, wearing chinos, a blue dress shirt, and a striped tie came around from his desk and shook hands with Sarah and Bob.

"I am pleased that Captain Blanchard has assigned me to the case. The Women's Club has been a special fixture in Calm Woods Cove for so long, and I don't want anything to happen to the club's unique reputation or to the reputation of Calm Woods Cove. We do want people to continue to feel safe walking all around our town.

"Sarah, let's get started. Please tell me your recollections of what happened last night at the Women's Club. State as many details as you can remember. Nothing is too trivial."

After Sarah gave her statement, Detective Smith picked up a sheet of paper. "Sarah, before I give you the report from the officers, I want to tell you that the officers cleaned up your office. You may use it again. Other than the mirror missing, there is just a small hole in the wall where the bullet was found."

"I thank you and your men for that," replied Sarah.

"Now, this is the report from the officers who responded to your call last night. One fact stands out. All the doors to the building were locked. Whoever fired that shot used a key to get inside. Who has keys to the clubhouse?"

Startled, Sarah replied, "Only five people have keys besides myself—First VP Laurie Johnson, Second VP Ruth Wilcox, Treasurer Peggy Lowe, Rental Manager Penny Shriver, and the custodian, Ralph Benson."

"Can you think of any reason why any one of them might want to frighten you or do you harm?"

"No, I feel that I have a very good relationship with all of them, and I consider all of them good friends."

"Also, we did a ballistic test on the bullet taken from the wall behind the mirror. It came from a .45-caliber handgun. Do you know if any of the key holders have a handgun?"

"No, I have never heard any of them mention owning a handgun."

"Well, it seems that the person who did the damage at the clubhouse had both a key and a handgun. I also want to mention that we found gunpowder on the office door frame which means that the shooter had to have been right outside the door and could have easily killed you. I am guessing though that the intent was to scare you rather than kill you."

Sarah was visibly shaken by all this. Detective Smith continued, "I'd like you to give all this information serious thought. Think about who might have a gun, who would want to scare you, and why would they want to scare you. Let me know immediately if you think of anything that might lead us to a suspect, and most importantly, be careful. Don't stay in the clubhouse alone even during the day. In the meantime, the five key holders will be contacted and interviewed. I intend to find out if any of them own a handgun. I'll let you know if I learn anything."

Suddenly, a thought popped into Sarah's mind, and she became quite distracted. "With last night's happenings, I almost forgot that we have a club day event tomorrow at 1:00 p.m. Should I cancel it?"

"No, but I would like to be there to explain what has happened and to ask the members for their help in solving this case."

"That is perfect," replied Sarah. "I am not sure I could handle answering questions about last night's disturbing events."

There being nothing else to discuss Bob and Sarah thanked Detective Smith for his help and left for home.

The next day, Sarah woke with a queasy feeling in her stomach. She really did not feel like going to the clubhouse. She had no idea what she should say to anyone about the bizarre incident. She was glad that Detective Smith was going to explain what had happened.

Detective Smith picked Sarah up at 12:45 p.m. and drove to the club. They entered the clubhouse through a rarely used side door adjacent to the stage to avoid encountering anyone. Members could not see them from the ballroom where they were enjoying coffee, tea, delicious pastries, and lively conversations. None of the conversations, however, were about what had happened at the clubhouse the night before. It appeared that no information about the incident had leaked out.

Shortly before the start of the business meeting, Detective Smith walked out to the center of the stage and called for quiet. He spoke for a few minutes describing the incident involving the shattered mirror and then fielded questions. When he ended the briefing, the hall was all abuzz. Those present could not believe what they had just heard. One member could be heard saying, "Someone shot and shattered a mirror in the clubhouse office while Sarah was there. That's unbelievable!"

Sarah then appeared on stage and all became quiet again until someone shouted, "Sarah, how are you? Were you hurt? Were you scared?"

"I am fine," she told her audience. "But please, if you can help solve the mystery, contact Detective Smith. Nothing like this has ever happened in the club before. It is truly distressing. I certainly hope it will be solved quickly."

Then changing the subject, Sarah continued, "In a few minutes, we will proceed with our regular business meeting and program." Sarah then disappeared behind the stage curtain.

Five minutes later, Sarah reappeared, rapped her gavel, and called the business meeting to order. She called upon club members to stand and recite the Collect for Club Women written in 1904 by Mary Stewart, a high school principal and women's club member. The Collect's words seemed especially pertinent given the happenings of the previous night.

"Keep us, O God, from pettiness, let us be large in thought, in word, in deed. Let us be done with faultfinding and leave off self-seeking. May we put away all pretense and meet each other face to face, without self-pity and without prejudice. May we never be hasty in judgment and always generous. Let us take time for all things: and to grow calm, serene, gentle. Teach us to put into action our better impulses, straightforward, and unafraid. Grant that we may realize it is the little things that create differences, that in the big things of life we are at one. And may we strive to touch and to know the great common human heart of us all. And, O Lord God, let us forget not to be kind!"

After the Collect, the members recited the Pledge of Allegiance. Following this, board members, one by one, gave their reports. Sarah then made a few remarks, closed the meeting, and the stage curtains were drawn.

Sarah was whisked off the stage by Detective Smith, and together they took seats in the audience to view the afternoon's program, "How to Dress Fashionably." Mary Lansing, the speaker, was introduced and appeared on stage. She was greeted with enthusiastic applause. She thanked the club members for their warm welcome and then proceeded with her talk. She began by saying, "Fashion can seem very elusive and only for the elite. However, putting together a fashionable wardrobe is easier than it seems. The most important thing is to always remember that clothes that you love and feel good in will boost your confidence." She then went on to give step-by-step tips as to what to do to put together a fashionable wardrobe.

As a special climax to the program, the speaker called various club members to the stage so she could use them to show off certain trendy accessories. Laurie Johnson, for example, was chosen to model scarves. For the finale, she called upon Sarah to help showcase some beautiful new lines of jewelry. As Sarah mounted the stairs to the stage, a strange squeaky sound was heard. Suddenly, the multicolored bright lights attached to a bar on the stage ceiling began blinking. The bar then started moving and swaying and soon crashed thunderously to the stage floor. This produced a loud popping of the light bulbs as they hit the floor and broke into a million pieces.

Sarah and the speaker, having narrowly missed being hit by the falling apparatus, ran from the stage. Someone turned off the switch which controlled all the lights in the ballroom and on the stage. Some members were paralyzed in fear while others were screaming and starting to get up to flee. Detective Smith was at the front of the stage in no time calling for quiet and telling everyone to stay calm and to remain in their seats. He called police headquarters for backup.

Within a few minutes, two crime scene investigators and three patrolmen appeared at the clubhouse. The Calm Woods Cove Women's Club was again a crime scene. The patrolmen cordoned off the stage with yellow tape for safety reasons and to protect any evidence from becoming contaminated. They also marked off an area that included the entire stage in hopes evidence might be found later.

While that was going on, Detective Smith and the two crime scene investigators readied themselves for the interrogation of the eighty members who had witnessed the catastrophe. Of the key holders, only one was not present—Ruth Wilcox was home sick.

It took an hour to individually fingerprint and question all the women and record their answers. The men found it interesting how many different descriptions of the afternoon's happenings they heard, but not one woman provided any information that would help solve what had occurred. The incident was baffling.

Once all attending members were questioned, Detective Smith addressed them, "Thank you all for your patience and help. I encourage you to report to me any information you might think of, no matter how trivial. It might just help solve this case." He then added, "You are all free to go home." The women happily applauded his words.

Detective Smith spoke with the officers who had been investigating the debris on the stage. He shared the information with Sarah. "Someone jury-rigged the light bar so that it would fall."

"Isn't that hard to do?" asked Sarah.

"No, the way it was done was easily accomplished and could be done by anyone."

Sarah was truly frightened now. *What was going on? Why was someone trying to cause havoc at the Women's Club? Was she the target, or was it the club?* She hoped Detective Smith would be able to come up with answers soon.

Before leaving to go home, Sarah looked for Ralph Benson to see how he had reacted to the incident. She expected to find him in the kitchen, but he was nowhere to be seen. She searched the entire first floor and upstairs of the clubhouse. Ralph was nowhere. She then went to the lower level. She found Ralph sitting in a lounge chair in the coatroom looking visibly upset.

"Ralph, are you okay?"

Startled, Ralph replied, "Sarah, that whole incident just terrified me. I was so certain that someone was going to get hurt. I could not look. I think the phone call the other night has truly left me spooked. I am sorry."

"Don't worry about it. Also, I'm happy to report that no one was hurt, only the light bar was damaged. The police have finished questioning all the women, but I think they might want to question you. Come back upstairs with me and talk to them. After that, you should go home and take it easy."

"Thanks, Sarah. I'll follow you upstairs."

Back in the ballroom, Sarah and Ralph parted ways. Ralph went to talk to the police and Sarah left for home.

Bob was already at home when Sarah got there. She gave him a kiss hello and then said, "Bob, guess what happened at the Women's Club today?"

"Another mirror got shot?"

"Not funny. The lighting bar hanging from the ceiling on the stage crashed to the floor, leaving just enough time for the program speaker and me to get out of the way."

"Wow! Was anyone hurt?"

"No, luckily only the light bar was damaged. The police said it had been jury-rigged to fall."

"Do they have any idea who might have done it?"

"They have no idea. They questioned and fingerprinted all eighty women who were at the club, but they did not learn anything that might help solve the incident."

"Boy, the Women's Club is certainly becoming a dangerous place to be."

"You are not kidding. I am not looking forward to going there again until the mirror and light bar incidents are solved."

"How did Ralph take all this?"

"Strange that you should ask. Just before I came home, I was looking all over the clubhouse for him. I finally found him sitting in a lounge chair in the downstairs coat room, looking visibly upset. He said that the light falling had terrified him. He thinks the call the other night has left him spooked."

"I feel bad for him. I hope he can get the call out of his mind. I am sure today's incident had nothing to do with him."

"I think you are right, but I am not sure what today's incident was intended to do."

"Sarah, enough about the Women's Club. How about going out for dinner?"

"Sounds like the perfect antidote to a disturbing day. Where do you suggest we go?"

"I feel like having a thick juicy steak. Let's go to Beef Galore."

"Sounds good. Give me a few minutes to freshen up, and I'll be ready to go."

"Great. I'll take Bella out for a quick walk in the meantime."

"Perfect."

After a fifteen-minute ride, Bob and Sarah arrived at Beef Galore. They were greeted by the hostess and asked whether they wanted to sit at a table or booth. They chose a booth. On the way to be seated, they saw Ruth and Paul Wilcox and went over to their table to say hello. After the usual cordialities, Sarah said, "Ruth, we missed you at the clubhouse today. We heard you were sick."

Slightly flustered, Ruth answered, "I felt sick this morning, but I am fine now."

"That's good. Did you hear about what happened at the club meeting today?"

"Yes, Peggy called me. You must have been terribly scared."

"Yes, I was. I am just incredibly grateful that no one was hurt."

"Yes, thank God."

"Well, we will let you finish enjoying your dinner. It was good to see both of you. Ruth, I'm glad you are feeling better."

"Thanks, Sarah."

"Hope to see you again soon. Enjoy your dinner," said Paul.

Seeing that Bob and Sarah had finished their conversation, the hostess came over and showed them to their booth. As soon as they were seated, Sarah said, "I can't believe Ruth is here. I wonder if she was the one who caused the havoc at the Women's Club today and then decided to play sick."

"I know you don't really believe that Ruth caused the havoc, but something is going on with Ruth and with Paul too. They just did not act like themselves."

"I agree. I wish I knew what was going on with them."

Bob responded, "Time to forget them and enjoy a good meal."

Bob ordered a sizzling eight-ounce filet mignon, a baked potato with sour cream, green beans, and a house salad. Sarah had a six-ounce steak, baked potato, broccoli, and a house salad. For dessert, they both had a hot fudge sundae.

Feeling invigorated after their delicious meals, they returned home to find Detective Smith waiting for them. "I'm so glad you are back. Sarah, I want you to avoid even going near the clubhouse.

What happened today proves that whoever is out to get you has a criminal mind. They are not thinking clearly."

"That is a scary thought," said Bob.

"Has anything new come to mind about today's incident?" asked Detective Smith.

"Yes. Bob and I just had dinner at Beef Galore and who did we see but Ruth Wilcox and her husband, Paul. Remember Ruth was the key holder who was not at the club today because she was supposedly sick. She did not look sick at all tonight. I asked her if she knew about the incident at the club, and she said Peggy had told her about it."

"That is very interesting. I think I will pay her a visit."

"Probably a good idea. Bob and I both thought Ruth and Paul acted rather strangely."

"I will leave you now. Remember, go nowhere near the Women's Club."

"Don't worry. I won't."

CHAPTER 3

The Message

Four days passed. Nothing new happened at the Women's Club, but then Sarah had not ventured anywhere near the clubhouse per Detective Smith's directive. Monday, however, she decided that she really had to go to the clubhouse. There were several forms she needed to fill out and checks which needed her signature. She called Detective Smith to let him know of her plan to go to the club and to ask him if he could accompany her or else send an officer to take her.

"Give me ten minutes, and I'll gladly pick you up," he responded.

Once inside the clubhouse, Sarah and Detective Smith went immediately to the club office where the shooting had taken place. Sarah was surprised to see that in place of the shattered mirror, someone had hung a floral print. Seeing the lovely flowers, Sarah was wondering who had been thoughtful enough to hang them there. Sarah began to relax a little. She went to her mailbox. There was a stack of papers and some envelopes in it. She took everything out, walked over to the desk, and sat down and began going through it. In the middle of the stack, she found this typed note: "The club was my last hope. Sarah, you have ruined everything. Now you must pay!"

Trembling, she showed the note to Detective Smith. "Well, we now know for sure that the other night's shooting, the incident on the stage, and now this note, point to you as the target. It also appears that whoever is out to get you is doing it because of something that happened in conjunction with the club. Although we can't count on this absolutely, it seems that any acts of retaliation will probably take place in the clubhouse. With that in mind, Sarah, I emphatically repeat, you must never come down here except in my company or in the company of someone from the Police Department."

"Don't worry. I would be too frightened to set foot in here without police protection."

"Sarah, please try to think of a reason why someone would have left such a hateful note in your box. Try to come up with someone who might feel wronged by something you did. Concentrate especially on the key holders or some other club member."

"I will, but right now I am too upset to think."

Sarah forced herself to continue looking through the rest of the stack on the desk. She filled out responses on two forms and signed payroll checks. She was then almost ready to leave with Detective Smith, but first, she wanted to check on Ralph. They found him in the ballroom setting up tables for a wedding.

"Sarah, Detective Smith, hello," said Ralph.

"Ralph, good to see you," said Detective Smith as he shook Ralph's hand.

"How are you doing?" asked Sarah.

"I am feeling much better."

"I'm so glad to hear that. Stay positive," said Sarah.

"Thanks, I will. Sarah, how are you doing?"

"I am pretty stressed, but hopefully, things will calm down soon."

"I am sure they will," said Ralph.

"Ralph, we should let you get back to work, said Sarah. "See you soon."

"Goodbye."

With that, Sarah and Detective Smith left the clubhouse. On the ride back to Sarah's house, Detective Smith reminded Sarah to try very hard to come up with a reason why someone would be so upset with her. Sarah promised to do so and then thanked Detective Smith for having accompanied her to the Women's Club. Once back home, Sarah took Bella for a walk and then went upstairs to her bedroom to relax for a while. She could not wait for Bob to get home. She was nervous and exhausted from the day's events. She wished that she would find that she was just having a bad dream. But a dream it was not. She fully realized that all that happened recently was real.

How could this be happening at the Women's Club? she asked herself. *There is no rhyme nor reason for it. I hope I don't have to go back to the clubhouse again until the recent happenings have a logical resolution.* With those thoughts in her mind, she fell soundly asleep.

About an hour later, she was awakened by Bob's kiss hello.

"Are you okay?" he asked.

"Yes, I'm just overwhelmed by what has been happening at the Women's Club. I went down there today with Detective Smith to do some paperwork, and in a stack of papers, I found a note telling me that I had been the last hope, but I had ruined everything and now I must pay. Whatever those words mean, I do not know."

"I'm glad Detective Smith was there with you. I am sure he will try to figure it out."

"I'm sure he will." Sarah then added, "There was something good that happened while we were there. Ralph told us that he is doing much better."

"I'm so glad to hear that. Now, Sarah, tell me what you would like to do tonight."

"Just stay home and relax."

"Tell you what, come downstairs, I'll fix you a drink and then put a couple of hamburgers and corn on the cob on the grill."

"Sounds great, and I'll put together a nice salad. Also, since the weather is so nice, I think we should eat out on the patio."

"Great idea. Maybe the deer will come join us."

Sarah laughed as she could feel her spirits lifting thanks to Bob's comforting touch.

For over a week, Sarah stayed away from the clubhouse, but then she received a frantic call from Penny Shriver, the rental manager.

"Sarah, I'm sorry to bother you, but a prospective client has an appointment to see the building this afternoon at five. I was planning on being there, but I have a sudden emergency and must leave now. I would cancel the appointment, but the client is flying in from

California as we speak. I have been trying to contact our custodian to ask him to fill in for me, but I have been unable to reach him. Could you possibly meet the client?"

"I'll be happy to do that. What is the client's name?"

"Bob Williams," Penny answered. "He may want to rent the ballroom and living room."

"Don't worry. I will give him a complete tour of the building."

"That would be perfect."

"Penny, I hope your emergency is nothing too serious."

"No, it is just something I need to take care of."

"Good luck and see you soon."

"Thanks."

After completing her conversation with Penny, Sarah telephoned Detective Smith to let him know of her need to go to the clubhouse.

"I'll pick you up at four forty-five," he quickly responded.

Detective Smith was true to his word, and he and Sarah pulled into the clubhouse parking lot at 4:53 p.m. They quickly walked from the car to the clubhouse back door. Sarah unlocked the door, and they went inside to wait for the client. At the dot of 5:00 p.m., the doorbell rang at the canopy entrance to the clubhouse.

"I imagine that's Mr. Williams," Sarah said.

She and Detective Smith went to the door and found Mr. Williams, a pleasant-looking, casually attired man with brown hair and glasses, probably in his late thirties waiting to enter the clubhouse.

After welcoming him and introducing themselves, Sarah, accompanied by Detective Smith, showed Mr. Williams around the rooms used for rental parties. First, they went into the ballroom a large room that exuded sophistication. It had twenty-five-foot ceilings, elegantly draped French doors on two sides of the room, and brass chandeliers and wall sconces. At the back and overlooking the room was a Juliet balcony lined with potted ivy plants. At the front of the room was a large stage, ample enough for a small orchestra to provide music for dancing on the softly polished wood floor. To the right of the stage, there was an attractive bride's room, and on the left side was a wheelchair-accessible bathroom facility.

"How many people can be seated in here?" asked Mr. Williams.

"Using tables and chairs, 220 people can be seated comfortably, with room for dancing. With an auditorium-style setup, 350 can be accommodated," answered Sarah.

Next, they walked through one of the sets of French doors which led to a stunning garden. It was filled with seasonal blooms, mature shrubs and trees, and lush green grass. A paver stone path led to a gazebo and stone bench. The atmosphere was one of sheer elegance and natural beauty.

"Weather permitting, the garden is a spectacular place for cocktails or for a wedding ceremony. Tables and chairs can be provided for this area," said Sarah.

The three then returned to the ballroom, and Sarah said, "Follow me," and led the two men across an elegant brick-floored foyer and into the living room. It was a stunning room with brass chandeliers and two antique fireplaces with finely detailed wood mantelpieces. Mirrors hung above the mantelpieces, and framed artwork decorated the walls. A beautiful faux oriental carpet in blue and burgundy tones was the finishing touch to the room.

"This is truly an exquisite room," said Mr. Williams. "How many tables and chairs can fit in here?"

"Six roundtables with eight chairs at each," answered Sarah.

Next, they visited the kitchen. Mr. Williams was impressed that it had all the amenities needed by a professional caterer.

"Do you have a caterer you are planning to use?" asked Sarah.

"No, we don't have anyone in mind. Can you suggest someone?"

"Certainly. I can give you our vendor list of caterers, florists, bands, etc. I think you will find everything you might need for your event on it."

"Thank you. That would be most helpful."

"Well, that's the first floor. We will now go upstairs," Sarah said invitingly. Upstairs, she showed Mr. Williams the balcony that overlooked the ballroom. The balcony led to a very large room with a fireplace at each end, framed prints on the walls, a parquet floor, and rustic chandeliers and sconces. There were no tables or chairs in the room, but Sarah told Mr. Williams that tables and chairs were available to be used there and on the balcony.

Sarah then led the men down beautifully carpeted stairs to the basement area. Mr. Williams was surprised to find several lovely sitting areas, along with a coat room and a men's and women's lounge. There was also a special space for children to play, watch TV, or enjoy a movie.

The tour ended, and everyone returned to the first-floor office where Sarah answered any questions that Mr. Williams had and gave him the official rental packet and vendor list. Satisfied with everything he had seen, Mr. Williams decided that he did want to rent the clubhouse on the date he had temporarily okayed with Penny. He gave Sarah a $750 security deposit check to hold the date and thanked her for her help.

"I will make sure Penny gets your check but be sure to call her as soon as you can so she can put together your contract."

"Of course. I definitely do not want to lose this place. I am planning a surprise fiftieth wedding anniversary party for my parents. They live in a neighboring town, so it will be most convenient for them to come here. I am sure they will love the Calm Woods Cove Women's Club."

"I hope so," responded Sarah. Goodbyes were exchanged and Mr. Williams went on his way.

"Such a nice man," said Sarah "I think Penny will enjoy working with him. Speaking of Penny, I want to put this check with a short note on her desk upstairs."

Detective Smith followed her upstairs and waited while she unlocked the rental manager's office. They entered the room, and Sarah was surprised to see that it seemed to be in a chaotic state.

I guess Penny didn't have time to straighten up before she left on her emergency, she thought. Sarah then walked over to Penny's desk. Her index finger began pointing at something, and while shaking, she let out an ear-piercing scream and then fell to the floor in a heap. Detective Smith rushed over to help her and then saw that on the floor behind Penny's chair was the custodian Ralph Benson slumped over in a pool of blood. It appeared that he had multiple wounds to the back of his head and torso.

Detective Smith called police headquarters and then picked up Sarah causing her to come out of her faint and then placed her on a chair in the hallway.

"Sarah, just stay here. Someone will come to help you in a few minutes," Detective Smith said.

About five minutes later, a large contingency of police and emergency personnel arrived on the scene. A friendly-looking policewoman was assigned to help Sarah. As soon as the policewoman approached her, Sarah asked, "How is Ralph Benson?"

The policewoman just shook her head and said, "Mr. Benson had already been dead for quite some time before you and Detective Smith discovered his body."

Just as Sarah was learning this, Detective Smith came to her side. "Sarah, are you okay?"

"Yes, but I think I will never forget the image of Ralph's bloody body lying on the floor, and I am certainly glad the client was not with us when we found him."

"Try not to think about it. Come on, let me take you home now so that my men can begin their work here."

Bob was already home when Sarah and Detective Smith arrived there. Detective Smith told him about Ralph Benson. Bob was astounded at what he was hearing.

"How could all this be happening at the Women's Club?" he asked.

Detective Smith spoke up, "Sarah, there has to be some connection between you and some club member and the murder of Ralph Benson. See if you can come up with a motive for the murder. Remember the note you found that said you must pay—perhaps this is the retaliation, perhaps not. Let's get together here, say, 10:00 a.m. tomorrow."

"That's fine," Sarah replied. "Thanks for your help. See you tomorrow."

After Detective Smith left, Sarah just fell apart sobbing uncontrollably. "Poor Ralph. Remember the phone call he had gotten frightening him about his job? We thought it was just a prank. I am now thinking it was not a prank. Maybe the one who threatened him is the one who actually murdered him. Perhaps we could have stopped this from happening if we had told Detective Smith about the call. This is so awful. I truly feel responsible for Ralph's death."

"Sarah, you cannot blame yourself for Ralph's murder. Whoever did this is a very sick person. Come, sit down. I'll fix us a drink. You have to relax," responded Bob, trying to comfort her.

Sarah and Bob had their drinks and a bit of dinner and then turned on the nightly TV news. The top story was, of course, the murder of Ralph Benson. The reporter began the story by noting that Ralph Benson had been found murdered that afternoon at the Calm Woods Cove Women's Club. He had apparently been shot multiple times at close range. According to the police report, there were no suspects and no clues. The reporter then asked, "Why would someone want to kill Ralph Benson, a kindly gentleman with many friends in the community and why would anyone choose to kill him in the Calm Woods Cove Women's Club?"

At this point, the camera zeroed in on the clubhouse, and the reporter remarked on the idyllic beauty of the historic building and repeated the often-repeated story of how back in 1928 the members of the club had raised the necessary funds to buy the land and eventually build the existing clubhouse. He then pointed out that now, so many years later, the clubhouse was still serving the Women's Club and the Calm Woods Cove community well. With a strained voice he added, "Hopefully, this will never change." He ended his report by extending his sympathies to Ralph's family and added that he hoped that Ralph Benson's murderer would soon be caught. He called on the viewers to contact the police if they had any knowledge that might help solve the murder.

After the news was over, Sarah turned to Bob, "Tomorrow I must tell Detective Smith about the phone call that Ralph had received."

"Yes, you must," responded Bob. Sarah began to cry, and Bob attempted to comfort her. She sat nestled in his arms for quite some time. Finally, they decided to retire to bed. Sarah fell asleep from emotional exhaustion as soon as her head hit the pillow.

Hopefully, she would awake fully refreshed the next day and ready to work with Detective Smith to come up with a killer.

CHAPTER 4

New Evidence

At 10:00 a.m. the next day, Detective Smith appeared at Sarah's door.

"Let's get busy. We've got to see if we can come up with a suspect before another murder takes place. Let's start by you telling me all about Ralph Benson," said Detective Smith.

"Ralph Benson has been the club's custodian for the last three months. Our previous custodian, John Stevenson, suffered a massive coronary four months ago. Club members, their husbands, and a cleaning service filled the void while we looked for a new custodian. We received eight applications for the job and decided to interview four of them. All of them had been recommended by a club member. Ralph Benson was one of the four, thought to be the best choice, and has—or rather, had—lived up to our expectations."

"Who was actually involved in the hiring process?"

"First VP Laurie Johnson and I did all the interviews together. I, as president, did the actual hiring."

"I have the feeling that someone is out to get you because of your choice of Ralph Benson for the custodial position."

"I should have already mentioned this. The night before the mirror was shattered at the clubhouse, Ralph had received a phone call threatening his job and insulting him with obscenities. I told him it was probably just a prank call, but that if it happened again, we would notify the police. He went along with this, and I presume that he did not receive any subsequent calls."

"From what you have just told me, it seems that everything that has happened is tied to the custodial position. Let's review all the candidates and who suggested them."

Sarah began, "First, we interviewed Frank Millard who was recommended by our treasurer, Peggy Lowe. He used to work at St. Andrew's Church where Peggy is a parishioner. He had surgery for lung cancer about a year ago and because his prognosis was not good, he lost his job at the church. However, he made a remarkable recovery, and his doctor okayed his working again. When he approached the church, he was told they could only give him sporadic part-time work. He really needs a full-time job, so Peggy suggested he interview for the club's position."

"Why didn't you hire him?"

"We had misgivings about whether he would be physically able to do the job."

Detective Smith then asked, "Who was your next candidate?"

"Raymond Garcia. He was recommended by Second VP Ruth Wilcox. He is the husband of her cleaning lady of ten years. Mr. Garcia had been working at the King's Castle restaurant until it closed nine months ago. He told us he wanted and needed a full-time job. We did not hire him because we weren't sure he would be able to communicate professionally enough with our club members and rental clients. His English is quite broken."

"Who was the third candidate?"

"Andrew Gleason. We heard about him through our rental manager, Penny Shriver. He was recommended to her by Elite Gourmet Caterers, used frequently by our rental clients for weddings. Mr. Gleason was looking for more money than we were able to pay, so our interview with him ended quickly."

"How about Ralph Benson?"

"Maureen O'Gara, a club member recommended him. He used to work in the high school her children attend. This year, the Board of Education turned the local schools' custodial needs over to a hotel chain's management corporation. The corporation brought in its own people. As a result, custodians like Ralph lost their jobs after many years of service to the school district and to the community. Ralph had worked at Calm Woods Cove High School for twelve years and was well known and well thought of by the parents and students alike. We hired him because of his affable disposition, and more importantly, because he caught on immediately to what we expected of him. And, I might add, we were not disappointed. We will truly miss him."

"Sarah, do you have any idea what Penny Shriver's emergency was, the day of the murder?"

"No, when I said to her that I hoped it was nothing serious, she replied that it was just something she had to take care of."

"That is a strange answer. It seems like she was hiding something. I think I will pay her a visit. Also, do you think she was upset about the hiring of Ralph Benson?"

"It is possible. If Andrew had been hired, Penny probably would have had more rental business coming her way because Andrew had lots of connections with caterers. She is not only paid a salary, but she gets a nice commission on every rental that takes place."

Detective Smith sighed and then said, "I will get busy looking at our list of suspects—Penny Shriver, Peggy Lowe, and Ruth Wilcox. They all have a vested interest in the custodial job. They all have a Club key, but not one of them has admitted to owning a handgun."

"I can't believe that Peggy or Ruth or Penny would be out to harm me or anyone else, let alone be a murderer. Bob and I socialize all the time with Peggy and her husband, Matt. I was instrumental in getting Ruth to join the Women's Club. Penny has been working as a rental manager for four years, and I have never had any problems with her."

"I'm going to do some digging and see if I can come up with anything that might cause any of these women to commit murder. If you can think of anything, let me know immediately."

"Of course. I can't wait until the nightmare is ended."

"By the way, since the club needs a custodian again, I would like to provide one. We have a number of retired police who would be more than happy to earn a little extra money, and at the same time, act as our eyes and ears."

"That's great. I have been in such shock over Ralph's murder that I had not even thought about our custodial problem."

"Also, you can let your clients know that a security guard will be present at all functions in the clubhouse until the murder is solved."

"The club and I much appreciate all your help."

"Well, I guess that is all for now. I shall get busy with what we discussed. Oh, can you give me a schedule of events taking place at the clubhouse over the next few weeks?"

"I don't have the schedule here at home, but our rental manager has all the info. I suggest you and anyone who is going to take over the custodial duties speak to her. She will be able to outline all the dates, needs, and duties for each clubhouse event."

"Is she at the clubhouse now?"

"Penny should be in her office now. She works Monday through Friday, from 9:00 a.m. to 3:00 p.m."

"I'll stop by the clubhouse on the way back to headquarters and speak with her. I will touch base with you tomorrow, but be sure to call me immediately if you learn anything or think of anything that might be helpful."

"Thanks again, Detective Smith, for all your help."

"All in the line of duty. Talk to you tomorrow."

After Detective Smith left, Sarah put in a call to Ralph Benson's family. A friend of the family answered the phone. Sarah explained who she was and asked how the family was coping and if there was any information about a planned memorial service. The friend replied that Ralph's wife and children were terribly upset and were presently not up to having a memorial service. However, they were planning to have one in the future. Sarah expressed her desire to attend a memorial service for Ralph and the friend promised to let Sarah know when it would occur.

"Thank you. Please give my condolences to the family and tell them to please call me if they need my help for anything," said Sarah.

"I will do that. Thank you for calling."

Next, Sarah called the Women's Club to let Lillian Callan know what Ralph's friend had said. She told Lillian that she would let her know when she learned more about the memorial service. If it was all right with Ralph's family, she hoped many members of the club would attend it.

For five days, Sarah and Detective Smith kept in daily contact, with nothing helpful coming to light. On day six, Detective Smith called, "One of my men has come up with some very interesting information. I would like to come by your house right now and fill you in on the details, if that's all right."

"That's fine," said Sarah.

"I'll be there in ten minutes."

Sarah felt very edgy as she waited for Detective Smith. What had he learned? She was not ready to hear anything negative about her friends, yet she hoped that whatever he had learned would help to bring this case to a swift conclusion. As this thought crossed her mind, the doorbell rang.

Detective Smith seemed extremely energized. "First, I want to tell you that I have eliminated Andrew Gleason and Penny Shriver as suspects. Andrew Gleason has a new job, and he's helping to promote rentals at the Women's Club so Penny Shriver will benefit."

"That is good news," said Sarah.

"I do, however, have some incriminating information for you. Do you know that Frank Millard is the husband of Peggy Lowe's cousin?"

"No, that is news to me."

"He is, and that is not all. It seems that Peggy's cousin, a woman named Janice, is Frank's second wife. Janice is twelve years younger than Frank, and they have three children all under the age of ten. Janice has a part-time job as a receptionist in a doctor's office, but she earns nowhere near enough to support the family. As a result of Frank's illness, they have been in terrible financial condition. In fact, Peggy and her husband have been helping to pay their utility and mortgage bills. I don't doubt that Frank, Janice, Peggy, and her husband all were counting heavily on Frank getting the club's custodial job."

"I am dumbfounded by all this. Peggy never said a word to me. She presented Frank's name to me as though she knew him only because he was a fellow parishioner at St. Andrew's Church."

"Well, if you ask me, Peggy Lowe has a perfect motive for wanting to relieve Ralph Benson of his position and also for being angry with you."

Before Sarah could respond Detective Smith continued. "There's more. We have come up with a motive for Ruth Wilcox. It seems her cleaning lady, Maria Garcia, and her husband also have been having very serious money problems. Since he lost his job nine months ago, things have become so bad that Maria has borrowed money from Ruth the past few months in order to pay the rent on their apartment. Ruth's husband is unaware of this, and Ruth is sure he will be quite upset if he learns about it. She naturally was counting on Raymond getting the club's custodial position so that she would be freed from her sense of financial obligation and save herself from the possible wrath of her husband."

"I can hardly believe all this. How do we find out which one or if one of them is guilty? I still find it difficult to believe that either Peggy or Ruth is a murderer."

"Well, I'm sorry to say that it seems that one of them is the guilty party. We just have to learn which one. I want you to put out a call that the club is again looking for a permanent custodian. Make sure Peggy and Ruth know that if their candidates are still interested, they will again be considered for the job, along with any new applicants. We will give it until next Tuesday and then see where we are."

After Detective Smith left, Sarah called the club office secretary, Lillian Callan, and asked her to contact Peggy and Ruth, and to articulate the fact that the club was again actively looking for a custodian.

Later that afternoon, Lillian reported back to Sarah that she had carried out her requests and that Frank Millard and Raymond Garcia were both still very much interested in the custodial position. Sarah thanked her for her help and asked Lillian to let her know immediately if anyone else applied for the job.

At the end of the week, only Frank Millard and Raymond Garcia showed an interest in the job. Sarah thought she should interview both men. She was just starting to call Laurie Johnson to let her know this when her phone rang. Lillian Callan was hysterical.

"Sarah, I just found an envelope on the desk with your name on it, and it was smeared with blood."

"Don't touch it or anything else on the desk. I will call Detective Smith immediately. He and I will be down shortly."

Within ten minutes, Detective Smith was at Sarah's door. He had also dispatched a squad car to the clubhouse. By the time Sarah and Detective Smith arrived at the clubhouse, the officers had already dusted the entire office for fingerprints. They also had opened the envelope in question. Inside was the following note: "Sarah, if you value your life, make the right choice this time." These words, too, were smeared with blood. Sarah began shaking.

"I wish the writer had identified herself. I still can't believe that either Peggy or Ruth is responsible for this, but it seems that one of them is."

"We will test the blood markings and see if we can learn anything from them," said Detective Smith. He then added, "Let me talk to my men for a few minutes and see if they have come up with any other evidence."

After a few minutes, he turned to Sarah, "Are you ready to go home?"

"Yes, I am more than ready to leave this place. When we get to my house, I hope you will come in and join me for a cup of coffee. I have something to show you."

"Thanks for the invite, and I must say you have piqued my curiosity."

Back home, Sarah settled Detective Smith in the family room and went to get coffee. She soon returned with a mug of coffee for each of them. She then showed Detective Smith a silver key ring with the initials PML on a circular charm. "While you were talking with your men in the office this morning, I just happened to look into the basket where Ralph has been putting items he finds while maintaining the building. This was in it. As you can see by the tag on it, he found it the morning after the shattered mirror incident in the hallway outside the office door. The initials PML stand for Peggy Monica Lowe."

Detective Smith showed great interest in this find. "This could be a real piece of evidence pointing to Peggy as the one behind all the havoc at the Women's Club, including the murder of Ralph Benson. Amazingly, it may turn out that Ralph helped to solve his own murder."

Just then, Sarah's front doorbell rang. "I can't imagine who that is. I'm not expecting anyone," she said.

As she went to the door, she looked outside but did not recognize the car in the driveway. She was a little afraid to open the door, but instantly became brave when she remembered that Detective Smith was in the next room. She unlocked and opened the door, and who should be standing on the doorstep, but Peggy Lowe and Ruth Wilcox.

How strange, she thought, *we were just talking about you*. Of course, she did not say that.

"We were passing by and saw Detective Smith's car in your driveway and thought we should stop by to make sure nothing else has happened at the Women's Club," said Peggy.

"Come on in and join Detective Smith and me for a cup of coffee," said Sarah.

"We would love to," said Ruth.

Peggy and Ruth followed Sarah to the family room where they exchanged greetings with Detective Smith. Once they were comfortably seated, Sarah brought them each a cup of coffee.

"Detective Smith, Ruth and I were concerned when we saw your car. Has anything happened at the Women's Club?" asked Peggy.

"There was some police business there this morning, but nothing for you to worry about. All has been handled."

"Not missing a beat, Ruth inquired, "What kind of police business?"

"I am not at liberty to discuss that information," replied Detective Smith. Peggy and Ruth both looked highly disappointed at his answer.

Moving on, Peggy asked, "Do you have any idea who murdered Ralph Benson?"

"We are still working on it." was Detective Smith's quick and succinct reply. Ruth and Peggy then began to speak at once, and as it turned out, they both wanted an update on the filling of the custodial position.

"We're not ready to make a decision yet. We're waiting to see if we have any other applicants," said Sarah.

"I don't know why you have to wait. The custodian position needs to be filled right now and you have two very good applicants. Ruth and I want you to make a decision now," Peggy blurted out in a very hostile tone.

"I'm sorry you feel that way, but I am not ready to make a decision yet. Anyway, we have a very good fill-in custodian from the Police Department, so we do not have to act too quickly," said Sarah.

Upset by this answer, both Peggy and Ruth got up to leave. They said goodbye to Sarah and Detective Smith, and Peggy added, "Sarah, I hope you come to your senses and make a decision very soon."

After the two women left, Sarah and Detective Smith both looked at each other and began laughing. They could not believe the theatrics they had just witnessed, but they knew something very serious was behind them.

"I think the case for Peggy being the murderer just keeps getting stronger," remarked Detective Smith

"I'm afraid so," said Sarah sadly. "What should we do now?"

"We'll wait until our Tuesday deadline as we had planned and see if there are any other applicants. Also, let's see if our guilty party does anything else to reveal herself. By Tuesday, at the latest, hopefully, we will have flushed out the killer."

"Tuesday seems so far off to me. Do you have any suggestions as to how I can distract myself from worrying?"

"Not really," Detective Smith replied. "Of course, there is always the chance that other applicants will come forward for the job, and then you and Mrs. Johnson will have to interview them. If this scenario comes to fruition, let me know the name or names of possible candidates. I will do a background check on whoever applies."

"That would be great. The Women's Club and I both appreciate all the help you give us."

"As I recall you said that before hiring Ralph Benson, eight men had come forward for the job. Have you heard from any of the four you dismissed early on?"

"No, none of them have applied. I think Ralph's murder is making potential candidates squeamish about the job."

"You are probably right, but don't get overly pessimistic. You never know. Try to stay calm and positive. All will be over soon, I promise you."

"Thank you. I feel better when I reflect on the fact that Detective Smith and his men at the Calm Woods Cove Police Department are guarding me and the members of the Women's Club."

CHAPTER 5

Day One

Sarah woke Thursday with a high level of energy and ready to do her best to keep all thoughts of the club out of her mind. She started by fixing a breakfast of juice, coffee, scrambled eggs, and toast for Bob and herself and then saw him off to work. While taking care of her breakfast dishes, the thought popped into her mind that in five days, if not sooner, she should know which of her two close friends was a cold-blooded killer. A shiver went down her spine as the image of Ralph's bloody body flashed through her mind. She shook herself.

Enough is enough. I mustn't dwell on the awful things of recent days or contemplate the future, Sarah counseled herself. *It is time to get busy. I have wanted to thoroughly clean the house for a while. It seems that this is the perfect day to start to do it.*

A peculiar thought then entered her mind. *If I survive until the killer is caught, I will have a nice clean home to resume my normal life in, and if I do not survive, no one will be able to say that I was a terrible housekeeper.* She laughed at her own wisdom.

Sarah dressed quickly in a pair of jeans, one of Bob's discarded shirts, and an old pair of sneakers. Full of purpose, she proceeded downstairs into the kitchen. She flipped on the lights and turned on the radio to a talk radio station. Sarah was counting on hard work and lively talk show dialog to keep her distracted from her problems.

The fridge was her first line of attack. She went hunting for things with expired sale dates. She tossed out some old cottage cheese, salad dressings that neither she nor Bob had been fond of, strawberries that were past their prime, and spinach salad leaves that looked like they had seen much better days. She cleaned the shelves and then rearranged the remaining items. As she looked at the results of her work, she thought to herself, *It is time to do some grocery shopping.*

Next, Sarah turned to cleaning out the kitchen cabinets. The hours flew by, and before she knew it was time for a lunch break. She fixed herself a grilled cheese sandwich and a glass of iced tea. While her sandwich was cooking, she went to check to see if the mail had arrived. It had and she was pleased to find no bills, but catalogs from three of her favorite stores.

These will keep me entertained while I eat, she thought.

The phone rang just as she sat down to enjoy her lunch. It was Bob checking on how she was doing. Sarah reassured him that she was fine, and he promised to be home by 6:00 p.m. for dinner.

Sarah had barely hung up when the phone rang again. She saw by the caller ID that it was Peggy. Though she was almost afraid to take the call, after five rings she did. Sounding cheerful and friendly, as she always did, Peggy began by apologizing for having rushed out so unceremoniously from Sarah's house the day before. "I had just been hoping that you were going to say that the custodial position was settled. But that is not why I am calling. Lillian Callan told me about the horrible incident with the note. I can't imagine such a thing happening at the club. Are you okay?"

Sarah reassured her that she was fine. Then Peggy got to the point of her phone call. "Matt and I were talking last night, and we both agreed that you and Bob need a pleasant diversion. We would like you to join us at the new restaurant in town La Bonne Vie for dinner Saturday night. We ate there a few weeks ago, and the food was outstanding. Also, they have an excellent dance band there on Friday and Saturday nights, and I know you and Bob love to dance."

Happily surprised by the invitation, Sarah responded, "Sounds wonderful. Let me talk to Bob tonight, and I will get back to you in the morning."

"Certainly. I do hope we will be seeing you Saturday. I'll talk to you tomorrow. Goodbye for now."

"Goodbye, Peggy. Thanks."

Sarah hung up the phone. She reviewed the conversation she had just had with Peggy. *Peggy can't possibly be the murderer. She sounded too normal. And what a great invitation!*

La Bonne Vie had opened in Calm Woods Cove about three months ago and was highly popular. Sarah and Bob had never been there. Sarah had frequently heard others talking about it and had been looking forward to the day when she and Bob could judge for themselves if all the rave reviews were justified. She hoped Bob would say "yes" to going. *Besides*, she thought, *such a public place should be safe*.

Excited by the turn of events, Sarah quickly finished her lunch and then returned to her cleaning efforts. By the time she finished, the kitchen was sparkling.

Bob arrived home at 6:05 p.m. and found Sarah busily preparing dinner. They kissed each other hello, and then Bob, holding Sarah out in front of him at arms' length, commented, "You look especially pretty and relaxed this evening. What's up?"

Sarah told Bob about her day and about her call from Peggy Lowe. "Bob, I just can't believe that Peggy is a murderer. The conversation I had with her was as natural as ever. I really would like to join Peggy and Matt Saturday night, if that's agreeable with you."

"I am in favor of going. Some of the guys at work have been talking about La Bonne Vie and they have aroused my curiosity. Before we accept, though, I think we should check with Detective Smith to see if he has any problems with our socializing with Peggy and Matt. Let me call him right now."

Bob made the call and then reported back to Sarah. "Detective Smith gives our plans his blessings. He suggested that we meet Peggy and Matt at the restaurant to avoid being alone with them. He also added that he and his wife will be at La Bonne Vie at the same time, just in case."

Sarah was delighted and looked forward to accepting Peggy's invitation in the morning.

CHAPTER 6

Day Two

Friday, Sarah woke in an upbeat mood. She was looking forward to calling Peggy to accept the invitation to join her and Matt for dinner at La Bonne Vie Saturday night. After enjoying breakfast with Bob and seeing him off to work, she thought that it was too early to call Peggy, so she decided to relax for a few minutes with a third cup of coffee and the morning newspaper. However, she had barely begun to enjoy her relaxation when the ringing of the phone shattered her silence.

"It's only 7:30 a.m. I wonder who's calling so early?" she muttered to herself as she hurried to answer. "Hello."

"Hello, Sarah, it's Peggy. I apologize for calling so early, but something has come up and I have to drive to Connecticut to see my parents. I'll be leaving in about ten minutes, but I wanted to check with you about Saturday night before I left."

"Peggy, Bob and I would be delighted to join you and Matt Saturday."

"That's great. Matt and I will pick you up at about seven. How's that?"

Inclined to say, "That's fine," but remembering Detective Smith's words, Sarah replied, "How about we just meet you at the restaurant at 7:30?"

Sounding rather surprised, Peggy answered, "Well, okay. I'll make the reservation for four under the name Lowe."

"Great. Say hello to your parents for me. See you Saturday."

"Yes. Goodbye."

After hanging up Sarah reflected on the call. *Peggy seemed kind of startled when I said we should meet at the restaurant. I guess she had just expected me to agree with her and when I didn't—well, I hope that is why. Please, Peggy, don't turn out to be a murderer.*

Now, enough of that. Today, I must just concentrate on organizing all the master bedroom closets and drawers and giving the room a thorough cleaning.

Sarah quickly tidied up the kitchen, went upstairs, and immersed herself in the project for the day. She first focused on her side of the closet and her bureau. She decided to purge all items she had not worn for at least three years. Before she knew it, she had a pile of clothing on the bed waiting to be recycled to a battered women's shelter.

At 11:00 a.m., Sarah was interrupted by a call from Lillian Callan telling her that the mail had just arrived and that there were two strange-looking letters in it. One was addressed, "To the President," and the other, "To the First Vice President."

"Shall I open them?" asked Lillian.

"No. let me call Detective Smith. I'll call you back."

Sarah quickly hung up and dialed Detective Smith. He told Sarah to call Lillian back and tell her that he was on his way to the clubhouse to pick up the unopened letters.

"Do you want me to go with you?" asked Sarah.

"No, just stay put. I'll be back in touch with you soon."

Sarah was feeling very anxious and thought to herself, *If only I wasn't such a mess from cleaning, I would be tempted to jump in the car and drive to the clubhouse. I hope Detective Smith gets back to me soon. Oh well, in the meantime, I had better get back to work, or Bob and I will have to sleep in the guest room tonight.*

One hour passed, then two. Just as Sarah was thinking to herself *Why have I not heard from Detective Smith*, the doorbell rang. Sarah looked out her bedroom window and saw that Detective Smith's car was in her driveway. She hurried downstairs and welcomed him.

"Sorry for taking so long getting back to you. I had the two letters dusted for fingerprints and had a long talk with the club custodian [policeman]. First, the letters. Take a look."

The two envelopes and letters were identical except that one was addressed, "To the President," and the other, "To the First Vice President." Next to the addressee's name on each envelope was a picture of a bouquet of red roses with the words, "Please help," around the flowers like a halo. The letters were written on copies of an unpaid and long-overdue bill from a utility company and said, "The job at the Women's Club is my last hope. I don't know what will happen, if I don't get it. Sincerely, Raymond Garcia."

After looking at the letters, Sarah turned to Detective Smith. "Raymond Garcia did not write these. I'm sure Ruth Wilcox did. She may be the murderer."

"We can't jump to conclusions. I talked to my man, Joe Finnegan, and he had some very interesting information. It seems that at nine this morning, Peggy Lowe was at the clubhouse and asking lots of questions about the custodial job. She wanted to know for how long Joe had been hired, and if the permanent custodial position was still available. When he told her it was, she told him all about Frank Millard. Joe said she became very animated and almost angry when she told him how Frank had been bypassed for the job on the last go-round. She said she hoped Mrs. Peterson and Mrs. Johnson would come through for Frank this time. And then she added that they had better and made a quick exit."

Sarah was dumbfounded and the expression on her face must have reflected this.

"So why do you look so distressed?"

"Peggy called me this morning and said she was leaving before 9:00 a.m. for Connecticut to visit her parents. Why did she lie to me? What is going on? Both Peggy and Ruth are acting like murderers. I just can't believe all this."

"Has anyone else applied for the job?" asked Detective Smith.

"No one."

"If that's how the situation remains, then Tuesday morning, we will have Lillian Callan call Peggy and Ruth. She will tell Peggy that she just heard that you and Mrs. Johnson are meeting with Raymond Garcia at 11:00 a.m. to offer him the custodial job. Then she will call Ruth and tell her that she heard that you and Mrs. Johnson are meeting with Frank Millard at 11:00 a.m. to offer him the custodial job. At 11:00 a.m. Tuesday, I believe our murderer will show up at the clubhouse."

"But today is only Friday. Can't we do something *now*?"

"No, let's stick to our original time frame. Try to have a pleasant weekend, Sarah. My wife and I are really looking forward to going to La Bonne Vie tomorrow night."

"Bob and I are too, but I am not sure I like the idea of having dinner with a murderer, if, in fact, Peggy is one."

"Call me if anything else comes up. Otherwise, I'll see you at La Bonne Vie."

"Thank you for all your help. See you tomorrow."

After Detective Smith left, Sarah returned to her bedroom. She consumed herself with putting it back in order while trying to digest the afternoon's revelations. Bob arrived home just as she was finishing the final touches. She greeted him with a big hug and kiss and then filled him in on the latest happenings. Bob's response to Sarah's outpouring was to try to cheer her up.

"I know exactly what you need after having had a day like you've had. I'm going to pick up a large pepperoni pizza and a bottle of wine. After dinner, I'll give you one of Bob Peterson's famous back massages."

CHAPTER 7

Day Three

Sarah and Bob loved Saturdays. They always took advantage of it being a non-workday by sleeping in. Today, they got up at 9:00 a.m. and were greeted by lots of sunshine and temperatures in the sixties. After a simple breakfast of juice, coffee, and croissants, they decided to venture to the bike trail for some exercise. The trail was not crowded, so they enjoyed a most pleasant ride.

They returned home at 1:00 p.m. to the phone ringing. Bob answered and was pleased to hear his daughter Amy's voice. As the youngest child and only girl, Amy grew up receiving special treatment from both her parents and her brothers. Happily, this did not tarnish her, and she developed into a lovely young woman, strikingly good-looking, intelligent, and with a most congenial personality, and in her sophomore year at Vanderbilt University.

"Hi, Dad. I just wanted to check in with you and Mom."

"Mom is here. Let me put you on speaker."

Sarah and Bob talked with Amy for about half an hour. She had lots of happy news to impart. In particular, she announced that she would be home for summer vacation in two weeks and that she had a job at a local department store waiting for her when she did get home.

"We're so proud of you," Sarah and Bob responded together.

Amy then asked, "How are things in Calm Woods Cove?"

Bob and Sarah told her about the murder at the Women's Club, but they did not mention that Peggy Lowe or Ruth Wilcox—her mother's friends—were the prime suspects. They didn't want Amy to worry needlessly when there was not a thing she could do to help the situation. On a happy note, however, they did mention that they were going to La Bonne Vie restaurant with the Lowes that evening and that they were really looking forward to it.

"You should be excited to go. I've heard that it is a spectacular place. Hope you have a wonderful evening," said Amy. After a few more pleasantries, the conversation ended.

I hope nothing happens to me that will prevent me from seeing Amy finish her schooling and get married and have children, etc., Sarah was thinking. Luckily, Bob interrupted her thoughts before they became too depressing.

"What's for lunch?" Bob wanted to know. Sarah fixed them each a bowl of tomato soup and a sliced turkey sandwich. While enjoying their lunch, they rehashed their conversation with Amy.

During the rest of the afternoon, Bob took care of some work he had brought home from the office, and Sarah did some gardening. Sarah had always loved gardening, and the space she had chosen in her yard to set up a garden had perfect conditions to grow all sorts of things. In one section, she was able to grow all her favorite flowers according to season, and in another section, her favorite herbs, spices, and vegetables. She and Bob thoroughly enjoyed their home-grown summer salads.

The hours passed quickly, and soon it was time to get ready for their big evening out. Sarah was feeling more and more apprehensive as the clock moved toward 7:30 p.m. She was wondering how she was going to be able to carry on a normal conversation, while the thought that Peggy might be a murderer lurked in her mind.

Maybe we shouldn't go, she thought. She expressed this to Bob, but he told her not to worry—what with eating, drinking, and dancing, all should go smoothly.

Sarah showered, did her hair, nails, and makeup, and then stood in her closet surveying her wardrobe. She finally chose an exquisite pale pink evening suit, for which she had matching shoes. Her jewelry for the evening included a pearl necklace, matching earrings, her diamond engagement and wedding rings, and a diamond watch. When Bob got a glimpse of her, he showered her with appreciative whistles.

"Mrs. Peterson, you look fantastic. Just keep a smile on that beautiful face and I promise all will go well this evening."

Since the ride to the restaurant would take no more than ten minutes max, Sarah and Bob decided to leave the house at 7:20 p.m. They arrived at La Bonne Vie, an old, lovely, refurbished mansion on the outskirts of Calm Woods Cove's business district. Bob pulled into the driveway at the restaurant and stopped the car at the valet parking sign at the main entrance. Bob helped Sarah out of the car, and they walked together into La Bonne Vie at 7:35 p.m. The place was bustling.

"This place really is a hot spot," Bob exclaimed. "Do you see Peggy and Matt anywhere?"

"No, I guess we should just ask for our table," replied Sarah. Bob spoke to the maître d' and they were escorted to a lovely table for two near a window.

"There seems to be some mistake. The reservations for Lowe were for four people," said Bob.

"Sir, if you and your wife will just wait here for a minute, I will go and check."

While waiting, Sarah and Bob took in the decor of the room. It was truly an elegant, romantic setting with the air of a French country inn. This, the main dining room, had a low-beamed ceiling, a wonderful stone fireplace, and windows that looked out on a beautiful garden filled with spring blossoms. The lights were very dim, and candles burned on each table which were set with white linen tablecloths and napkins.

The maître d' returned carrying an envelope. "Are you the Petersons?" he asked.

"Yes," Bob and Sarah responded in unison.

"Well, then this is for you. After reading it, you can tell me what you would like to do."

"Thank you," Bob replied. He then opened the envelope and read what was inside.

Dear Bob and Sarah,

I am sorry, Matt and I will be unable to join you this evening. We are stuck in Connecticut with my parents. We knew you were looking forward to enjoying La Bonne Vie, so we decided to leave you this note at the restaurant rather than at your home. Please be our guest and just put your bill in our account. Enjoy yourselves.

Love,
Peggy

"Can you believe this? What is going on?" Sarah asked after Bob had finished reading.

"Sarah, I can give you no answers at this moment. We just must accept what the note says. If it is true, they are being extremely solicitous and generous."

"Yes, and that scares me."

"Do you want to stay? Of course, we will pay our own way. Or would you rather go home?"

"I'd like to stay now that I don't have to worry about facing Peggy. I can have a wonderful evening with my favorite beau."

"Good decision."

Bob then called the maître d' over and told him that they loved their table and would be staying for dinner and dancing. The maître d' then handed them each a copy of the menu, pointed out the wine list on the table, and then walked away. Soon a waiter came and asked if they would like something to drink while they studied the menu and disappeared to get each of them a glass of Chardonnay. He returned with their wine and a basket filled with warm rolls and butter and a plate of crudités with an accompanying dipping sauce.

After perusing the menus for quite some time, Bob and Sarah finally made their appetizer and entrée choices. Sarah selected a spinach salad with goat cheese, cranberries, and walnuts in a champagne vinaigrette, and salmon sautéed with Belgian endive, shallots, white wine, lemon, and butter. Bob chose escargot bourguignon—snails in garlic-parsley butter—and grilled filet mignon in a creamy morel mushroom brandy demi-glace. With their dinners, Sarah and Bob enjoyed a bottle of their favorite pinot noir wine. Before indulging in dessert, Bob and Sarah took to the dance floor. The music was wonderful and encouraged everyone to get up and dance. When Bob and Sarah finally took a break for dessert, they each ordered coffee and chose selections from the dessert trolley.

Bob and Sarah thoroughly enjoyed their evening out. They had to agree that La Bonne Vie merited all the rave reviews that it received. The food and service were indeed four-star, and Sarah and Bob danced tirelessly all evening to the terrific music played by the band. As the evening wore on, their problems became less and less important, at least for the time being anyhow. They even almost forgot all about Peggy and Matt and probably would have had they not run into Detective Smith and his wife on the dance floor. Detective Smith seemed concerned when he heard about the missing Lowes.

CHAPTER 8

Day Four

After not getting to bed until after 1:00 a.m., Bob and Sarah took advantage of it being Sunday morning, slept in, and went to an 11:00 a.m. church service. Afterward, they stopped to pick up bagels and cream cheese at Calm Woods Cove's popular gourmet bagel shop. When they arrived back home, they found Detective Smith waiting for them.

"Detective Smith, what brings you here on a beautiful Sunday?" asked Bob.

"I am sorry to disturb your Sunday, but I have something to tell you."

Sarah responded, "Come on into the house and join us for a cup of coffee and some bagels and cream cheese."

"I'll take a rain check on the bagels, but a cup of coffee sounds great."

Once the three of them were comfortably settled at the kitchen table, Detective Smith explained why he had turned up at their doorstep. "I didn't want to say anything last night and spoil your evening, but Peggy was down at the clubhouse again late yesterday afternoon talking to Joe. She mostly repeated what she had said to him the day before. I don't believe the Lowes ever went to Connecticut. Why she is feeding you that line, I don't know. But something strange is going on. I came by to warn you to be careful. In case you hear from either of the Lowes, do not consent to get together with them. Put them off. Tuesday will be soon enough to deal with Peggy. I tell you frankly that I am leaning toward believing Peggy is our murderer. On that happy note, I am going to leave you and let you enjoy your Sunday afternoon."

After Detective Smith left, Sarah and Bob both had terrible feelings of anxiety. For a while, neither one spoke, but finally, Sarah said, "I can't wait for all this to be over, but I am still finding it very difficult to deal with the fact that Peggy, one of my closest friends, is seemingly a murderer. Deep in my heart, I can't believe it, but I guess my feelings of friendship for her are clouding my judgment."

Her words were followed by the ringing of the phone. Neither Bob nor Sarah wanted to answer it for fear that it might be Peggy or Matt.

"Let's just let the answering machine take the call," Bob said to calm Sarah and himself as well.

They listened to the machine. First, they heard the machine's message and then their twenty-five-year-old son, Ryan's voice. Relieved, Bob jumped up and picked up the phone. Sarah and Bob talked to their son for thirty minutes, but they did not mention the murder at the Women's Club. Ryan, however, did have some exciting news to tell them.

"Mom and Dad, I have met someone very special. Her name is Elizabeth, and I am hoping that you are not busy next weekend so I can introduce her to you."

Bob responded, "That is wonderful."

"Why don't the two of you come out on Friday night and spend the weekend with us," Sarah suggested enthusiastically.

"That's just what I was hoping you would say. I would like Elizabeth to see what great parents I have and to see where I spent my formative years. Calm Woods Cove is so different from where Elizabeth and I have apartments in New York City. It is great living in the city especially since our jobs are here, but Calm Woods Cove is really a special place."

"I'm glad you feel that way, Ryan," Bob said. "Your mother and I will be looking forward to seeing you and meeting Elizabeth Friday night."

Sarah and Bob wished Ryan a good week and then ended the conversation.

"How exciting," Sarah said beaming. "Wouldn't it be nice to have a wedding in the family?"

The phone then rang again. Caught up in the happiness of the moment, Sarah almost picked up the receiver. The answering machine came on and a subdued woman's voice was heard. It was Ruth Wilcox. She left a message.

"Sarah, this is Ruth Wilcox. Please give me a call when you get a chance. I was just wondering what is happening with the custodial position at the club."

"Thank God, I caught myself and didn't answer the phone. I would not have known what to say to her. Also, thank God for answering machines. They certainly do come in handy. Just think if we did not have an answering machine, we might have missed out on Ryan's great news."

"Before the phone rings and elevates our blood pressure, let's give Michael a call and see if he has anything interesting to tell us," Bob suggested. He dialed his son's number. On the sixth ring he turned to Sarah, "I guess he's not home."

He was about to hang up when he heard Michael's voice, "Hello."

"Michael, it's Dad. I was just about to hang up."

"I just came in from jogging. Is there anything wrong?"

"No, your mother and I just talked to your brother, and we thought that while we were by the phone, we would give you a call to see how you are doing."

Bob and Sarah talked to Michael for about twenty minutes. They learned that he was fine and enjoying his last weekend before starting his summer clerking job for a law firm in New Haven, Connecticut. He told them that he had talked to one of the students who clerked for the firm the summer before and was told to expect long working hours.

"Have you met Ryan's girlfriend?" Sarah asked him.

"No, I haven't."

"If you have any free time next weekend, stop home, and you can get to meet Elizabeth."

"I would like to, but who knows what free time I will have. I will try to call you Thursday night and let you know what I am doing."

Bob and Sarah said goodbye to their son and wished him well in his clerkship. It was now almost three o'clock.

"Let's get out of the house before the phone rings again," suggested Bob.

"Good idea. Do you want to go to the antique show and sale at the Community Church in Silverton?" asked Sarah.

"Sounds like a great idea to me," answered Bob.

Bob and Sarah spent a couple of hours at the show and sale. There were about seventy-five dealers and a wide assortment of merchandise. In the end, they made one purchase. They bought an antique pendulum clock for the mantelpiece in their family room. They looked forward to hearing it chime on the hour and half hour.

On the way home, they stopped at one of their favorite little restaurants, the Cookery, for a quiet Sunday dinner. They slipped into a booth, and a waiter immediately brought them each a glass of water and menus. He asked if they wanted anything besides water to drink. They both ordered iced tea. The waiter soon returned with their drinks and took their orders. Sarah ordered a turkey burger deluxe with sweet potato fries, and Bob, a cheeseburger deluxe with regular fries.

When Sarah and Bob arrived home about 8:00 p.m., they found the light on their answering machine blinking. There were two messages. The first was from Detective Smith. He was just checking in on them and if all was okay when they received the message, they could wait to call him in the morning. The second message was from Peggy Lowe's mom.

"Sarah, this is Monica Porter—Peggy Lowe's mom. I would appreciate it if you would give me a call as soon as possible."

"I better call Detective Smith and let him know about this."

Sarah dialed his number. He answered on the first ring. Sarah told him Monica's message. He told her to go ahead and call her and then call him back. He was very curious as to why Monica was trying to contact Sarah.

Sarah promptly hung up and dialed Monica's number. She answered and sounded pleased that Sarah had returned her call so quickly. "Sarah, I called you because you are one of Peggy's closest friends. Peggy has been acting very strange lately, and I was hoping you might know why."

"Monica, I agree. Peggy's behavior has seemed rather strange lately, but I cannot give you any explanation for it. If I learn anything, I will be most happy to let you know, and if you learn anything that I can help with, please let me know."

Sarah ended the conversation. She dialed Detective Smith's number. She reiterated her conversation with Peggy's mother. They both commented that it was going to be awful if they had to tell Monica that her daughter was a murderer.

Detective Smith then quickly changed the subject. "I hope you and Bob enjoy your Memorial Day holiday tomorrow. Do you have any special plans?"

"No, we plan to stick pretty close to home."

"Good. I will be available all day if you need me for anything."

"Thank you. Hope you enjoy your Memorial Day too."

CHAPTER 9

Memorial Day

Sarah and Bob awoke to perfect weather for Memorial Day—sunny with just a few clouds and temperatures in the low seventies. They planned to attend Calm Woods Cove's Memorial Day ceremonies beginning at 10:00 a.m. in Peace Park. Sarah, as president of the Women's Club, was originally going to speak at the celebration, but Detective Smith thought it would be better if someone else represented the club, given the ongoing murder investigation. He had, however, given his okay on their attending the activities, as long as they kept a low profile.

Sarah and Bob each dressed in patriotic colors and then went to the kitchen to enjoy breakfast. Bob insisted on making his special scrambled eggs, turkey sausage, toast, juice, and coffee. Sarah loved being waited on and gave Bob a huge thank-you hug and kiss. They cleaned up the kitchen together, and then Bob asked Sarah, "Are you up to jogging to the park?"

"Yes, the exercise will do me good."

After locking up, they began the jog to Peace Park. A large crowd had already assembled to observe the ceremonies. Sarah and Bob looked around and finally found a good spot from where they would be able to see and hear all the proceedings. At precisely 10:00 a.m., a parade of local officials, clergymen, and representatives from local volunteer organizations, veterans, police, and fire personnel and boy and girl scouts entered the park and came to rest before the memorial erected by the town to honor war veterans. It was now surrounded by beautiful flowers donated by local organizations including the Women's Club. A speakers' platform had been set up. The first to approach the podium was Reverend Paul White from the First Congregational Church who offered an opening prayer. One of the veterans then led all in the recitation of the Pledge of Allegiance and the singing of the "Star-Spangled Banner." He was followed by at least eight other speakers, including the mayor of Calm Woods Cove, and Pauline Wright, the third vice president of the Women's Club. She read a beautiful poem in tribute to all veterans. The ceremonies concluded with a prayer offered by Rabbi Isaac Kantar and the firing of a cannon. Ceremonies lasted about an hour and fifteen minutes.

As they were leaving the park, Sarah and Bob ran into a few of their friends including some from the Women's Club, but they only engaged in brief exchanges with them.

"Let's stop at the Cinnamon Tree for lunch before we jog home," suggested Bob.

"Good idea, but I do hope you have money with you. Since we jogged down here, I left all my money and credit cards at home."

"Not to worry, I've got my wallet."

Sarah and Bob walked several blocks to the Cinnamon Tree, a lovely small restaurant. The owner of the restaurant, whom they knew very well, seated them at a window table that overlooked the main street. The waiter had just served them iced tea when Ruth Wilcox and her husband, Paul, came walking along the sidewalk and waved to them. Then before Sarah and Bob could have counted to ten, Ruth and Paul were standing by their table.

"Just stopped by to say hello," Ruth said and then continued, "Did you get my messages?"

"Yes," Sarah responded, "but it was too late to call you last night, and since today is a holiday, I just planned to get back to you tomorrow."

"I'm glad we ran into you then. What is happening with the club's custodial position?"

"It is still in limbo. Detective Smith advised me to put any decision off for the time being."

"Please let me know as soon as you are ready to make a decision. We won't disturb you any longer. Enjoy your lunch and the rest of the day."

After bidding Ruth and Paul goodbye, Sarah let out a sigh of relief.

"Great answer you gave her, Sarah."

"Thanks, I don't even know how I came up with it. Nothing like blaming everything on Detective Smith. I hope Ruth doesn't start pressing him about the job."

"She might. I thought she seemed a bit unfriendly. And poor Paul, she did not even give him a chance to speak."

"Come to think of it, you are right. Usually, Paul would have told us about the latest intrigue happening in Calm Woods Cove."

"Maybe the only intrigue is happening at the Women's Club."

"Well, that is certainly enough intrigue. I hope for everyone's sake it gets solved soon."

With those words, the waiter brought them their lunch. Each had ordered a triple-decker sandwich, but Sarah had chosen chicken and Bob, roast beef. They enjoyed their choices while engaging in only happy conversation. They decided all Women's Club talk was strictly forbidden. As a result, their lunch was relaxing and most enjoyable. Afterward, they strolled along the main street, stopping to gaze at the shop windows. Sarah spotted a lovely red sweater she might be interested in buying at one of her favorite stores. She wished she could have had a better look at it, but all the stores in town were closed in tribute to Memorial Day. She made a mental note to herself to come back another day to try it on. She and Bob finished their tour of the stores and then jogged a most circuitous route home.

Arriving home, they found a yellow plastic bag hanging on their front doorknob.

"I'm afraid to look inside of it," said Sarah.

Bob lifted the bag off the nob and reached inside. He pulled out a small beautifully wrapped box and an envelope. "Should we open the envelope or the box first?" he asked.

"The envelope, I guess, but let's first go inside and sit down," Sarah responded.

Once seated at the kitchen table, Bob tore open the envelope and found this note:

Dear Sarah,

> Just back from Connecticut. My mother was cleaning out some things and she came upon this. She and I both would like you to have it. Hope you enjoyed La Bonne Vie. Talk to you soon.
>
> Peggy

Sarah shook her head, "Boy, she is good. She really makes you want to believe she went to Connecticut."

"She sure does. But hurry up and open the box. I am really curious to see what is in it."

Sarah picked up the package and carefully untied the purple ribbon. She then removed the pretty floral wrapping paper and lifted the lid of the box. Inside was an antique cameo brooch.

"This is magnificent. Why would she give me such a beautiful piece of jewelry? I really don't understand how to respond to this."

"I think we had better call Detective Smith and inform him of our day's events," Bob said.

Detective Smith, upon hearing of the incident with Ruth Wilcox, indicated that he was impressed with Sarah's handling of it and that he was ready to deal with Ruth if she called him. He was, however, as confused as Sarah and Bob were about Peggy's gift.

"For the moment, do nothing. I will give this some thought. If by chance she calls, Bob, you talk to her and tell her that Sarah is unavailable to come to the phone. If she mentions the gift just thank her and tell her that Sarah will call her back as soon as she can."

"Fine. Hopefully, we will not hear from Peggy today."

"Give me a call later tonight and even sooner if anything else major happens."

When Bob got off the phone, he found Sarah holding the cameo in her hand and staring at it.

"This is so beautiful. Why would she give it to me? I wonder if her mother even knows she was planning to give it to me. I wonder when she got it from her mother—if, in fact, she did—since we know she did not go to Connecticut. So many questions! I sure do wish I knew what was going on with Peggy."

Bob filled Sarah in on the conversation with Detective Smith, and then they decided to play some tennis to distract themselves from the problems at hand. After tennis, Bob suggested they stop at Ice Cream Treats on their way home.

"I say wholeheartedly yes," responded Sarah. "What would Memorial Day, the start of summer, be without ice cream?"

When they got to Ice Cream Treats, there was quite a long line.

"I guess many great minds are thinking alike," said Bob.

Surprisingly, the line moved along quickly, and before Bob and Sarah knew it, they were being served. Bob ordered a three-scoop chocolate ice cream cone and Sarah, a cone with two scoops of butter pecan ice cream with chocolate sprinkles.

Tennis, ice cream, and the fact that they received no further communications from either Peggy or Ruth helped the rest of their Memorial Day wind down quietly.

Bob put in a call to Detective Smith about 10:00 p.m. After he learned that all was well, Detective Smith asked to speak with Sarah. He told her to call the clubhouse early the next morning and check with Lillian Callan to make sure there were no new applicants for the custodial job. If there were still none, then she was to set into motion the procedure by which hopefully the murderer of Ralph Benson would be caught.

After speaking with Detective Smith, Sarah began to feel quite uneasy. She was overcome with dread at the thought of having to face the next day's events—whatever they turned out to be.

CHAPTER 10

D Day

Sarah woke up Tuesday feeling sick to her stomach. She had lain awake practically all night, rehashing in her mind the gruesome murder of Ralph Benson and wondering which of her two friends was going to prove to be his murderer. She finally fell asleep at about 5:00 a.m. In no time at all, the alarm was ringing. It was 6:30 a.m. and time to start the day.

An hour and a half of sleep—how am I ever going to get through this day? she asked herself. *Maybe I should call Detective Smith and delay the outcome. I do not think I am up to knowing which of my two friends is a murderer. I'll see what Bob thinks.*

She forced herself out of bed and went downstairs to fix breakfast. Bob came downstairs shortly thereafter. "Bob, I was thinking maybe I should call Detective Smith and ask if we can delay today's events."

"Sarah, you don't want to do that. Then you will have everything hanging over your head."

"I guess you are right."

"Listen, Sarah, I'll be right here with you. I cannot possibly go to work today and leave you to deal with a murderer."

"Oh, Bob, thank you. I am a wreck. I wanted you to stay home, but I felt that I was just being a weakling and should not impose on you."

"Imposing upon me, you are not. I know that I can trust Detective Smith to do all that he can to protect you. But I also know that I would not be able to concentrate on anything at work while worrying about you. And I would not be able to live with myself if anything happened to you because I was not here."

Just then the phone rang. It startled both of them. *Who could be calling at this early hour*, Bob thought as he went to answer it. "Hello."

As Bob listened to the caller a look of shock came over his face.

"Bob, what's the matter?" Sarah asked. Bob did not answer her but continued listening in silence to the person on the other end of the line.

"Bob, please tell me what is going on," Sarah pleaded.

Finally, Sarah heard Bob say "I will fill Sarah in. If there is anything we can do for you, let us know. We will talk to you later." He then hung up the phone.

"What is it? What's wrong?" Sarah asked.

For several seconds, Bob just stood still as if in shock. He was going over in his mind how he was going to tell Sarah what he had just learned.

"Bob, are you all right? What has happened?"

"Sarah, sit down. I have some awful news. That was Matt Lowe on the phone. He and Peggy had a horrible argument late last night. Peggy went out of the house and took off in her car. It seems as if she was headed for her parents' house in Connecticut. She never made it there. She lost control of the car and smashed into the center divider of Route 95 and flipped over. Her vehicle immediately became engulfed in flames. Peggy was pronounced dead at the scene of the accident."

"What! Peggy is dead! How can this be happening? There must be some mistake. They are sure it was Peggy's car?"

"Yes, they are sure. The registration papers were in the glove compartment and not damaged in the fire," answered Bob.

"This is too horrible a nightmare. I don't want to believe it," Sarah exclaimed. Tears welled up in her eyes. Bob put his arms around her, kissed her forehead, and held her comfortingly as she began crying.

Sarah and Bob just sat holding tightly to each other for a good long while. They were both so stunned by the news of Peggy's death that it was as if they were paralyzed and were unable to either speak or move.

The ringing of the phone, however, finally forced them to break apart. Bob went to answer it. It was Detective Smith. He was calling to see if they were ready to put into motion the plan for the day. Bob repeated for Detective Smith the phone conversation he had had minutes before with Matt Lowe. He went on to say that he and Sarah were in total shock over Peggy's death. Detective Smith also seemed dazed by this latest development.

"I extend my deepest sympathies to both you and Sarah on the loss of your friend. Her death, however, may be a godsend. All signs, so far, had pointed to Peggy as the murderer of Ralph Benson. Now you and Sarah will not have to witness her actual apprehension for that crime. I am going to do some investigating into her accident. I want to make sure that it was just an accident. I will also continue my search to see if there's any further evidence that might substantiate the murder case against Peggy. I will keep in touch with you."

Bob told Sarah the details of what Detective Smith had said. "In one way, I hope Detective Smith learns some incriminating information about Peggy, and in another way, I hope he doesn't. It would be so nice to have this murder cleared up, but I am not ready to accept that Peggy was a cold-blooded murderer. Peggy and Matt have been such great friends to us. It would truly hurt me to learn that Peggy murdered Ralph Benson. And poor Matt—to not only lose his wife, but then to later learn that she was a murderer. No, that is all too much," said Sarah.

"Sarah, I find it intriguing, that Detective Smith said he was going to investigate to make sure what happened to Peggy was just an accident. I wonder what he is thinking. Does he suspect foul play? What do you think?"

"I cannot even go there. I want to believe that it was just a terrible accident, nothing more."

Sarah and Bob decided to eat a quick breakfast and then to dress so that they would be ready to help Matt if he called. He had told Bob that he had contacted his two children at college and told them of their mother's death. Alex was a freshman at the University of Colorado, and Katie, a junior at Stanford University. They were both getting immediate flights home and would need to be picked up at Newark airport. Sarah and Bob expected to help with this.

Also, Sarah needed to call members of the Women's Club to tell them about Peggy's death as soon as she knew more about the funeral arrangements. In preparation, she worked out a calling chain she would activate as soon as she had this information. She wanted to make sure that all the members of the club knew of Peggy's death. She hoped that many of them would be present at her memorial service. Over the years, Peggy had done much for the Calm Woods Cove Women's Club. She had been the type of member every club sought. She had been friendly, enthusiastic, and eager to give of her time and efforts. The Calm Woods Cove Women's Club would truly miss Peggy Lowe.

About 10:00 a.m., the phone rang. It was Matt Lowe. Sarah answered, "I am so sorry. I still cannot believe Peggy is gone. How are you and the kids doing?"

"Not great as you can imagine. I just came back from the Greer Funeral Home. We will have a wake tomorrow in the afternoon from two to four and in the evening from seven to nine. The funeral will be Thursday at 10:00 a.m. at St. Andrew's Church."

"I will be sure to see that the information is passed on to the Women's Club members. Peggy was a very special member of the Women's Club, and she will be truly missed. There are also a few non-Women's Club members that I will contact too. And if you can think of anyone you want me to call, please let me know. I will be happy to do it"

"Thank you for all your help. I know Peggy loved the club, and she had so many good friends, like you, there."

"Yes, she did," responded Sarah and she could feel tears well up in her eyes.

"Sarah, another reason for my call is that I have a favor to ask of you and Bob. I am leaving soon for Connecticut to pick up Peggy's parents and bring them here to stay. Katie is arriving at Newark airport at 2:05 p.m. and Alex at 2:45 p.m. Would you and Bob be able to meet them there?"

"Of course. We'll be glad to do that."

Matt gave Sarah the flight information. After exchanging a few more words, Sarah and Matt ended their conversation.

Sarah told Bob about the conversation and then proceeded to put the calling chain of the members of the Women's Club into action. The first call Sarah made was to Lillian Callan. Lillian was extremely distressed when she learned of Peggy's death. She and Peggy had been very close friends. Sarah explained the calling chain she had designed and asked Lillian to help with it.

After Sarah made her calls, she and Bob had a quick lunch and then left for the airport. The trip to Newark airport was a breeze.

"I guess we are traveling at the right time of day. The traffic is unbelievably light," remarked Bob.

"Hopefully, it will be the same on our way home," said Sarah.

Arriving at the airport, Bob parked the car in short-term parking, and then he and Sarah walked the short distance to the arrivals building. They looked up at the arrivals board and saw that Katie's flight was now scheduled to land at the same time as Alex's. They decided that Bob would find Alex and Sarah, Katie, and then they would meet up at the car. The plan worked well, and they all arrived at the car almost simultaneously.

Alex and Katie hugged each other for a long time. As would be expected, they were both quite visibly upset. Sarah and Bob tried their best to be comforting and answer their questions during the easy ride home.

"Mr. and Mrs. Peterson, do either of you know why my mother was heading to Connecticut at such a late hour? Was there some problem with my grandparents?" asked Alex.

"We have no idea. I think you best ask your father that question," answered Sarah. "Hopefully, he can explain what triggered her late-night trip."

Bob could tell that Sarah was getting upset answering questions about Peggy's accident, so he decided to take over. "Katie, do you have any questions?"

"Yes, I have lots. My dad did not give me much information about the accident. How many cars were involved?"

"Only your mom's. She hit the center median, causing the car to roll over, and then her car erupted into flames."

"Did anyone witness the accident?"

"No, but a truck driver passing by, saw the wreck, and called 911. When the police arrived, there was nothing they could do for your mom."

With that, Katie began sobbing. Alex pulled his sister over toward him and put his arm around her. They stayed in this position, comforting each other, for the last twenty minutes of the ride to their house. There were no more questions.

Bob pulled into the Lowes' driveway just as Matt was arriving with Peggy's parents. Within minutes, everyone was hugging each other and crying. Sarah and Bob spent an hour at the Lowes' house and then returned home to call their own children to let them know of Peggy's death. All three of them said that they would come home for the funeral. Sarah and Bob made a few more calls to let some additional friends know of Peggy's death.

It was now almost 6:00 p.m. Sarah decided she would take Bella for a walk and then return to fix dinner. Bella had been quietly lying on the family room couch. She jumped up with joy and came running when Sarah called her. When she arrived at Sarah's feet, Sarah picked her up and gave her a hug. Bella responded by licking her face. Sarah put on Bella's leash and the two of them went for a nice long walk. When Sarah and Bella returned, both seemed to be quite refreshed.

Sarah was just looking into the fridge to decide what to prepare for dinner when the phone rang. Bob answered it. It was Detective Smith.

"Bob, if it is possible, I would like to stop by your house now. I have something to tell you and Sarah, and I would rather do it in person than on the phone."

"Certainly, that is fine."

"What is fine?" asked Sarah.

"Detective Smith is coming over now. He has something he wants to tell us in person."

"That makes me very nervous."

Within ten minutes, Detective Smith was at their door. Bob let him in, and the two men joined Sarah in the family room. Detective Smith began, "I have been talking all day with the Connecticut police. I suggested to them that foul play might have been involved with Peggy's accident. At this suggestion, they immediately impounded the remnants of her car and did some exploring. They found residual pieces of something heavy that seemed to have been attached to the brake line that may have eventually worn through and severed the brake line. This is what probably caused Peggy to lose control of her car and propelled her into the guardrail."

Detective Smith took a pause waiting to see if Bob and Sarah had anything to say. They were speechless. Detective Smith continued, "Hypothetically speaking, I think Peggy jury-rigged her own car. I think she did it because she didn't want to face being charged with the murder of Ralph Benson. By dying in the car crash, she would have people's sympathy, not people's wrath. I am sure she did not expect anyone to suspect or to find out what she had done."

Bob reacted first. "How sure are you that the brake line was jury-rigged? Given the amount of damage done to the car couldn't the brake line have been damaged during the accident?"

"It is possible but highly unlikely. At this point, I'm sticking to what I have already told you, but I will continue to investigate the accident."

"I hope you find out that Peggy did not cause her own death," said Sarah. "I do not think she would do such a thing."

"Well, I hope that is true. Please let me know right away if you hear anything related to Peggy's accident."

Bob and Sarah assured him that they would and then they saw Detective Smith out. Bob put his arms around Sarah and hugged her tightly. He knew that she was terribly upset by what Detective Smith had just intimated.

Bob whispered in her ear, "I am sure Peggy did not cause her own death."

"Bob, thank you. You always know what to say to me."

Bob then leaned over again and whispered, "I am starved."

At that, Sarah began laughing, "I am sure you are. Let's go find something to eat."

They settled on some chicken noodle soup and grilled cheese with home-baked chocolate chip cookies and ice cream for dessert. Of course, Bella also joined them feasting on her own special food in her bowl on the floor by Sarah's feet. Dinner was most pleasant since no discussion of Peggy's death was allowed while they ate.

After dinner, Bob and Sarah cuddled up on the couch with Bella nestling right by them and watched an episode of *House Hunters International*. They allowed themselves to be transported to Puerto Morelos, Mexico, a fishing village just twenty minutes south of Cancun and one of the oldest communities on Mexico's Caribbean coast.

"I think we should move there," said Bob. "We need some relaxation and Puerto Morales seems like the perfect spot for relaxation—a place to get away from it all and experience the simple Caribbean life."

"Sounds perfect to me. Let's go," responded Sarah and then laughed.

"But since we can't get there right now, let's take Bella for a walk," said Bob.

In agreement, Sarah got Bella's leash and then Bella led them on a twenty-minute tour of the neighborhood. When they returned, the phone was ringing. Bob answered and was happy to hear his daughter's voice. Bob put her on speakerphone.

"Mom, Dad, how are you doing?"

"We are both fine," Bob answered.

"I am glad. I wanted to let you know that I am planning to be home tomorrow to go with you to the visiting hours at the funeral home in the evening. I really want to see Alex and Katie. I feel awful for them."

"That is very nice of you," said Sarah. "When should we expect to see you?"

"Probably around 5:00 p.m."

"That works well. See you then."

"Thanks, Mom and Dad. I love you."

"We love you too," Sarah and Bob said in unison and hung up the phone.

"That was a nice way to end our day," said Sarah.

"I agree. I hope you are relaxed enough now to get a good night's sleep."

"I hope so. I will try to keep my thought processes in off mode."

Thankfully, both Sarah and Bob fell blissfully asleep

CHAPTER 11

Incriminations

Sarah and Bob awoke to the ringing of the telephone at 7:49 a.m. They had forgotten to set the alarm the night before and had overslept for more than an hour. Bob picked up the receiver. It was Detective Smith. He wanted to meet them as soon as possible at police headquarters. Bob told him they would be there in about an hour and then he thanked him for having awakened them.

"I wonder why he wants to see us. Did he give you any hints?" asked Sarah.

"No, and I really didn't ask. I just said we would meet him in about an hour."

Sarah and Bob quickly readied themselves for their meeting with Detective Smith. They arrived at police headquarters at 9:00 a.m. and found Detective Smith waiting for them in his office. After the normal cordialities had been exchanged, Detective Smith spoke, "Have a seat. I asked you to come down here this morning because I have something to show you." He then opened a desk drawer and lifted out a plastic bag. Inside the bag was a semi-automatic .45-caliber handgun.

"This was found in the storage compartment between the driver and front passenger seats in Peggy Lowe's car. The crew that went over the car almost missed it because the body of the car was so badly mangled. But luck was with us, and they did. The gun was tested for fingerprints and a ballistics test was done on it. The results found that the only fingerprints on it belonged to Peggy Lowe. The bullets matched the one taken from the wall in the clubhouse office and the ones used in the murder of Ralph Benson."

Sarah and Bob sat in stunned silence, but then, what was there to say? Peggy Lowe, their good friend—may she rest in peace—seems to have been a cold-blooded murderer. What had driven her to commit such a deed? And did she kill herself to cover up her crime, wanting always to be held in high esteem by others? After several minutes of silence, Detective Smith broke in, "When I asked Peggy if she had a handgun she had said no.

"You were her close friends, did Peggy ever mention to you that she had a gun?"

Sarah and Bob both nodded no. Detective Smith then went on. "We know that Peggy really wanted Frank Millard to get the job at the Women's Club to solve some financial problems. It seems, though, that Peggy must have been under some other great pressure to cause her to react in such a violent way. Can you think of anything else that was bothering her?"

Sarah and Bob both shook their heads no.

"Perhaps Matt Lowe can enlighten us. I think I will pay him a visit this morning and see if he can shed some light on his wife's actions," said Detective Smith.

"Are you going to tell him that you have evidence which proves that Peggy murdered Ralph Benson?" asked Sarah.

"Not today, I think it is best to wait until a day or so after the funeral service. Peggy Lowe certainly can't cause any further harm now."

"That's true," Sarah said somberly. "I feel so awful for Matt and the kids and for Peggy's parents. Peggy's dad has a heart condition, and I'm afraid of what this news is going to do to him and to her mother too. Peggy was an only child, and even as an adult has played a large part in her parents' lives. They're really going to miss her."

"Do either or both of you want to come with me to the Lowes'?"

"I would like to come with you," answered Sarah. "Maybe I can be of some help. I would also like to hear what Matt has to say about Peggy."

"I wish I could join you, too, but I have a business meeting at 11:00 a.m., which I would rather not reschedule," Bob interjected. "But, Sarah, I will meet you back at our house about 2:00 p.m. so we can go to the funeral home together."

"I like that," Sarah responded.

"I don't think there's anything else that we can accomplish here, so we might as well get going," Detective Smith said giving the signal for all to exit his office.

Once outside, Sarah and Detective Smith said goodbye to Bob and then made their way to Detective Smith's car. Ten minutes later, the two of them found themselves at the Lowes' front door.

Detective Smith rang the doorbell, and within seconds, Peggy's mother opened the door.

"Sarah, Bob, why hello. Come in," and then said, "But you're not Bob."

"Monica, I would like you to meet Detective Smith. He is in charge of the investigation into Peggy's accident."

"Detective Smith, I'm pleased to meet you. Have you learned anything that might help explain the cause of my daughter's terrible accident?"

"No, but I was hoping that perhaps if we all put our heads together, we might be able to come up with some answers."

"Come, let's join the rest of my family. Everyone is in the den."

Sarah and Detective Smith followed Peggy's mother into a lovely large room with chestnut wood paneling and a wonderful stone fireplace. Matt, Alex, Katie, and Peggy's father, Ed, were all absorbed in reading either a book or a newspaper. As the others entered the room, they stood up to greet them. After Sarah introduced Detective Smith, he offered his condolences. He then explained the reason for his visit.

At first, all expressed the same sentiment that they couldn't understand what had happened. Peggy was a good driver. She had never been in an accident, nor had she ever received a traffic summons. Sarah conveyed the idea that maybe she had lost control of her car trying to avoid a collision with another vehicle.

Detective Smith said, "Probably that will never be known. The accident occurred so late at night that there was not much traffic. As far as presently known, no one observed the accident itself. A truck driver came upon the accident sometime after it happened, and he was the one who called police."

Wanting to direct the conversation, Detective Smith continued, "What I would like to know is why Peggy was traveling so late at night. Where was she going? What was her state of mind?"

Peggy's mother turned toward her son-in-law, "Matt, you were the last one to see Peggy. I have wanted to ask you these questions, but I have not been able to bring myself to speak the words."

"I have been so upset, Monica. I wanted to tell you and Ed and the kids what had happened that night before the accident, but I have been overcome by guilt and shame. I can now explain what happened that night."

"Matt, would you like me to leave so you can discuss this privately with your family?" asked Sarah.

"No, Sarah. Stay. You were Peggy's closest friend, and I consider you and Bob to be like family. You have given Peggy and me and our family great support over the years."

"Thank you for that," Sarah said.

Matt then began his recitation of the events of the night of the accident. "I must say I am not proud of my actions. I was tired and upset after having spent three hours paying bills and going over bank statements. I was most annoyed with Peggy because recently, I had asked her to cut back on her spending, but I found that she had spent more than ever. There were numerous bills for clothing, jewelry, makeup, and decorative items for the house. As soon as I mentioned these items, Peggy became very defensive, and before we knew it, we were embroiled in a horrible argument. Finally, she said that she could not take it anymore and that she was going to her parents' house. I tried to stop her by telling her that it was too late, that I was sorry, and that I was sure we could work things out. Her answer was that she needed to get away for a while and that after she had calmed down and thought things over, she would contact me. I decided that maybe she was right, that it would be a good idea for us to be apart for a while. I never envisioned her getting into an accident. I would do anything to turn the clock back."

Matt then began to cry. Everyone just sat still for at least five minutes after Matt had finished his confession.

Finally, the silence was broken by Peggy's mother, "Matt, I do not blame you for Peggy's accident, but I do have some questions to ask you. Recently, I have found Peggy's behavior to be rather strange. She has seemed very preoccupied and worried about something. Do you know what has been bothering her?"

"I know that she was very worried about her cousin Janice. She had not wanted to worry you, but Janice and Frank have not been doing well financially. It has been very hard for them especially since they have three small children. Things have been so bad that Peggy and I have been lending them money to help them cover their mortgage and utility payments. We have been happy to do this, but we have been hoping Frank would get the custodial job at the clubhouse. Peggy definitely was on edge waiting to hear whether or not he would get the job."

"I am so sorry to hear about Janice and Frank," Monica said and then turned to her husband. "We will have to give them a call and see if we can help them."

Ed nodded yes.

"Does anyone have anything else to add?" Detective Smith asked. No one did. "Then I won't bother you further. Again, I offer my condolences to all of you."

Monica thanked him and then invited Detective Smith and Sarah to stay to enjoy lunch which the women at St. Andrew's Church had brought the family. Detective Smith turned down the invitation, but Sarah was happy to accept as long as someone could give her a ride back home at 1:30 so that she could change before going to the funeral home.

"I can drive you," Matt replied.

After bidding Detective Smith farewell, all adjourned to the dining room for lunch. For the most part, very little was said during lunch and what was said had nothing to do with what had been discussed with Detective Smith. Shortly after lunch, Matt drove Sarah home, as promised. They engaged in only light conversation.

Sarah was ready to go to the funeral home when Bob arrived home. She filled him in on the events of the morning as they drove downtown. They both agreed that Peggy's family was going to be devastated to learn that she had murdered Ralph Benson.

"Now that Peggy is dead and no longer a threat to anybody, why can't the fact that she murdered Ralph Benson just be kept quiet? It'll be so much better for everyone," Sarah said.

"I understand what you are saying, but I'm not sure Detective Smith will agree with you," Bob said as he pulled into the parking lot of the funeral home.

The parking lot was already three-quarters full. Once inside, Sarah and Bob were immediately met by many familiar faces. They quickly joined Peggy's family and helped to welcome and thank those who had come and to introduce them to Monica and Ed Porter. Shortly after 4:00 p.m., the last visitors left. Matt thanked Sarah and Bob for all their help and invited them to join his family for dinner. Sarah and Bob, however, declined and went home to wait for Amy and to rest a bit before returning to the funeral home at seven o'clock.

Amy arrived home at 5:00 p.m. just like she said she would. Bob and Sarah were so happy to see her. Getting to visit with her provided some cheer in what was otherwise a truly solemn day. Bella was also very, very happy to see Amy. When she was home, she always gave Bella lots of special attention.

Bob, Sarah, and Amy had a light dinner and then headed to the funeral home. Twice as many people visited the funeral home in the evening as had visited in the afternoon. Detective Smith and his wife were among the visitors as were many members of the Women's Club. Sarah was very pleased to see that so many club members had come to pay a final tribute to Peggy Lowe. Sarah thought to herself, *Peggy deserves their attention. She had been a good friend to many of them. And the Calm Woods Cove Women's Club owes much to Peggy Lowe. I just wish that it wasn't true that she murdered Ralph Benson.*

As soon as Amy spotted Alex and Katie, she hurried over to them. All three joined together in a group hug. Sarah was happy to see Amy reaching out to Alex and Katie. She knew that they needed support now and would need it even more when it was revealed that Peggy murdered Ralph Benson. She was glad that Amy was going to be home over the summer. She hoped she would have time to get together with Alex and Katie.

Shortly after nine, Bob, Sarah, and Amy said goodnight to Matt, Alex, Katie, and the Porters and headed back home.

"How did Alex and Katie seem?" Sarah asked her daughter.

"Alex seems to be handling things pretty well, but Katie is having a hard time with all of it. I think it is hitting her harder because she and her mom were so close. Katie is really going to miss her mom. I am glad though that she is extremely fond of her grandmother so that should help. It is just too bad that the Porters live in Connecticut."

"Their house is only about an hour and a half away so hopefully Katie will be able to visit with her grandparents fairly often," said Sarah.

"That would really be good for all of them," added Bob.

Completely changing the subject, Sarah asked, "Who would like some ice cream? I found a new flavor—Espresso Explosion. I think it is delicious."

"Count me in," said Amy.

"And me too," added Bob.

After Amy tasted her first bite, she said, "You are not kidding. This is so delicious."

Bob, too, had to concur with her. After indulging in Espresso Explosion, Sarah and Amy decided to take Bella for a walk. They invited Bob to join them, but he said he had to check on some work-related items.

It was a beautiful evening, and Sarah and Amy really enjoyed their mother-daughter time together. Bella enjoyed it too. She got to see Frenchie, a large poodle that lives in the neighborhood. The two dogs appeared to favor each other.

When Sarah, Amy, and Bella returned to the house, it was almost ten. "I am really beginning to feel completely exhausted. I think I shall head off to bed. I need to be at my best for Peggy's funeral. I am reading a tribute to her," said Sarah.

"I didn't realize that you were going to do that. Can I see what you're going to say?"

"Certainly. Let me get it."

Sarah returned with her written tribute. Amy read it and tears welled up in her eyes. "Mom, this is wonderful. Peggy would be so happy with what you have said about her."

"Thank you. I'm so glad you approve. I just hope I can keep it together while I read it."

"I am sure you will."

Having finished his work, Bob went looking for his two best girls. He found them hugging each other.

"What's up?" he asked.

"I just read Mom's tribute to Peggy. I think it is wonderful and was giving Mom a hug to show her how grateful I am to have such a special mother."

"How about a group hug?" said Bob. "I don't want to be left out."

"A group hug is definitely called for," answered Amy. "Dad, you know that I think you are one terrific father."

Bob kind of choked up at Amy's words.

Noticing this, Sarah thought to herself, *I am so lucky to have three great children whom I get to enjoy. Why hadn't Peggy cared more about her children? Perhaps, if she had, she would not have murdered Ralph Benson. Oh, Peggy, how could you have done such a loathsome deed?*

"Mom, what are you thinking about? You seem to be a thousand miles away."

"Oh, nothing. I think I am just ready to drift off to sleep."

At that, Amy said goodnight to her parents, and everyone went off to bed. All three of them fell asleep immediately. They were all physically and emotionally exhausted. Even Bella, after she received her goodnight hugs from Bob, Sarah, and Amy, was happy to get into her cozy and comfortable dog bed. She slept at the foot of Bob and Sarah's bed and kept a protective eye on them during the night.

CHAPTER 12

The Funeral

Thursday, June 2, was a dreary, rainy day.

The weather fits my mood, Sarah thought to herself as she finished dressing for Peggy Lowe's funeral. It was 9:15, forty-five minutes before the start of the service. Bob and Amy were ready to go and sitting downstairs waiting for Ryan and Michael to appear. At 9:30, they both did and after being warmly welcomed by their parents and sister, all left for the church.

St. Andrew's Church was a beautiful medieval, gothic-style stone church with a seating capacity for one thousand worshippers. Not surprisingly, the church was almost filled to capacity for Peggy's funeral. Lots of flowers adorned the altar area and a picture of Peggy had been placed by the podium to be used by those giving eulogies.

At 10:00 a.m., the church bells began to chime, signaling the start of the service. Everyone in the church stood as the strains of "A Mighty Fortress is Our God" emanated from the organ and the choir. The officiant of the service, Reverend William Boyd, led the funeral procession down the center aisle of the church. Directly after him came two honorary pallbearers. Sarah recognized them immediately and was somewhat surprised at Matt's choice of pallbearers. They were Ruth Wilcox's husband, Paul, and Lillian Callan's estranged husband, Bruce. They were followed by assistants from the funeral home who carried the coffin, and then Matt, Katie, Alex, and Monica and

Ed Porter. Ending the procession was another couple accompanied by three small children. At first Sarah was wondering who the other couple was, but then it dawned on her that it was Frank Millard and his wife, Janice.

Sarah thought to herself, *What will happen to them now that Peggy is dead? I wonder if Frank will still want to work at the Women's Club?*

Once the family got to the front of the church, they placed a pall, a rich velvet cloth on the coffin and then went into the pew ahead of Bob, Sarah, and their children. Reverend Boyd asked everyone to be seated and offered words of greeting first to the Lowes, Porters, and Millards, and then to the rest of the congregants. This was followed by the choir singing a group of psalms and Alex reading an excerpt from his favorite passage in the Book of Wisdom: "The souls of the righteous are in the hand of God and no torment will ever touch them. In the eyes of the foolish, they seem to have died and their departure was thought to be an affliction and their going from us to be their destruction, but they are at peace."

Alex ended his reading by saying, "Mom, I hope you are at peace. I do believe you are." His words caused the church to be filled with reflective silence.

After several minutes, it was time for what was the most touching part of the service. Several people came forward to give their own special tribute to Peggy. Reverend Boyd spoke first and emphasized what a wonderful parishioner Peggy had been at St. Andrew's. She had always been available to lend a helping hand. Next, Katie, in a tear-choked voice, read a poem she had written about her mother. The poem extolled Peggy's virtues as a mother, teacher, and friend to her children and expressed how she and her brother would dearly miss her. Lastly, Sarah presented a glowing description of the woman she considered to be one of her closest friends and an invaluable member of the Calm Woods Cove Women's Club. During this part of the service, sobbing could be heard coming from various parts of the church.

The choir then sang "The Lord Is My Shepherd." As the last verse was being sung, Reverend Boyd approached the coffin and blessed it. He offered up prayers for Peggy and asked the congregants to say their own prayers for her. He then concluded the service and invited everyone to join in the procession of cars forming to escort the hearse to a nearby cemetery. This signaled the choir to begin singing the recessional hymn "Abide in Me" while everyone processed out of the church. First Reverend Boyd led the honorary pallbearers, followed by the coffin being carried by the funeral home assistants and then Matt, Alex, Katie, Monica and Ed Porter, and Frank and Janice Millard and their three children. Matt and the Porters waited outside the church for a while to briefly thank those who had attended the service.

A very long procession of cars, with headlights on, followed the black cars of the funeral establishment and entered the driveway of the cemetery and finally parked near the site of the burial plot. There were rows of chairs set up around a grave that was covered with a white cloth. Floral tributes that were brought over from the church and funeral home were set around the gravesite.

After everyone had assembled, Reverend Boyd spoke. "My friends, we have come together today to bury our dear sister, Margaret 'Peggy' Lowe, and to commit Peggy to her final resting place. We gather to comfort each other in our grief and to honor the life Peggy led—a life that was full of hope, happiness, laughter, and love… through good times as well as in bad. This is the way we will always remember Peggy." At this point, many tear-filled faces could be seen.

Following the prayer, Reverend Boyd read a passage from Scripture. He then invited everyone to join him in a brief period of silent prayer which was followed by the lowering of the coffin into the ground. Reverend Boyd offered a few special words of consolation to Matt, Alex, Katie, and Peggy's parents, and then asked everyone to join him in saying the Lord's prayer. After the coffin was in the ground, dirt was shoveled over it by family members. The service ended with the singing of "Amazing Grace." Before dispersing, most in attendance approached Matt and his family and Peggy's parents to express their sympathies which were gratefully received.

After the service, Sarah and Bob and their children were invited back to the Lowes' house where members of the Women's Club had prepared a luncheon for the grieving family and their close friends and relatives. Sarah and Bob stayed for a couple of hours and then returned home. Ryan, Michael, and Amy stayed a while longer chatting with Alex and Katie. They rehashed funny high school memories.

When the three of them finally arrived back home, Ryan and Michael only had a short time to visit with their parents. Before leaving, Ryan discussed with his parents the previously planned visit he and Elizabeth were going to be making to Calm Woods Cove. It was decided to postpone their visit for a week so that Sarah and Bob could recover somewhat from the events surrounding Peggy's death. Michael was happy about the new plan. He said he thought he would be able to come too. He really wanted to meet Elizabeth, the new female in his brother's life. And Amy, not wanting to be left out, promised to try her best to be home then also. Ryan and Michael were then given an upbeat sendoff.

Amy's flight back to Vanderbilt was not until the next morning, so she was able to spend the evening with her parents. Sarah especially was very happy that her daughter would not be rushing off. She needed someone to divert her attention away from the nagging thought in her mind—*Peggy Lowe was a cold-blooded murderer*—but she did not want to voice this thought while her daughter was around. In fact, she hoped that her daughter would never have to learn the truth.

Sarah, Bob, and Amy spent a pleasant evening together despite the circumstances of the day. At Bob's suggestion, they called in an order to their favorite Chinese restaurant, and Amy went to pick it up. She returned with a large bag filled with containers of General Tso's chicken, sesame chicken, sweet-and-sour chicken, brown and white rice, and fortune cookies.

Sarah took a fortune cookie right away and opened it. It said, "Your life is very dull. You must make changes." Sarah laughed heartily, as did Amy and Bob.

After dinner, Bob turned on the local TV station. Peggy's funeral was the lead story. The network began with the story of Peggy's accident and asked that if anyone had witnessed it to please notify the Connecticut State Police. Next, a reporter on site in Calm Woods Cove focused on the details of the funeral. He showed a lovely photo of Peggy, plus photos of the Lowes and the Porters. Seeing this, Sarah felt especially sad.

"I am going to truly miss Peggy," she said and began to cry.

Amy came over and put her arms around her mother. Sarah felt a little better. As Bob turned off the TV at the end of the story on Peggy, the doorbell rang.

"Who could that be?" said Sarah.

Bob accompanied by a barking Bella went to answer the door. Detective Smith was on the doorstep.

"Bob, sorry to bother you, but I just learned something very interesting and since I was in your neighborhood, I decided to take a chance that you were at home. Is Sarah here?"

"Yes, and our daughter Amy. Please come in."

Bob and Detective Smith went to find Sarah and Amy in the family room. Amy was introduced to Detective Smith and then all sat down to hear Detective Smith's news.

"Did you see the TV report on Peggy?" asked Detective Smith.

"Yes, we did," replied Bob.

"Well, a woman called into the Connecticut State Police. She told them that she had talked with Peggy on the night in question at a rest stop on 95. Peggy told her she was on her way to see her parents and was about thirty minutes away from their house but had felt so tired that she had to stop to get coffee. The woman said that when Peggy left the rest stop, she seemed very alert so she was surprised to learn that Peggy had crashed soon thereafter."

"That seems to squash the idea that Peggy wanted to kill herself," said Sarah.

"Yes, I agree," responded Detective Smith. "Now we will just have to figure out what did happen to her brake line."

"Something happened to Mrs. Lowe's brakes?" asked Amy.

"Yes, but now it appears that the brake line damage happened as a result of the accident, not before."

Sarah interjected, "There had been a question floating about that perhaps Peggy was trying to kill herself because of family problems, but it seems that theory has no validity. I'm so happy about that."

"I will keep you updated on anything else we learn. By the way, how are the Lowes and the Porters doing?" asked Detective Smith.

Sarah answered, "They got through the wake, the funeral, and burial as well as can be expected, but I'm worried about them now as they get back to normal life. I think it is going to be extremely difficult for them. Peggy's parents, I think, will be affected the most. Matt has work, and Alex and Katie have school, but the Porters are used to having Peggy visit them all the time."

"Katie was talking about getting a summer job in Connecticut near her grandparents," said Amy. "I think that would be wonderful for the Porters if she were to do that."

Everyone agreed. Detective Smith was now ready to leave.

"I will disturb your evening no longer. I will be in touch."

They all walked him to the door, thanked him for his good news, and bid him a good night.

"I'm so glad he stopped by to tell us that news. I feel so relieved," Sarah sighed. "I wonder if anyone else will come forward with information relating to the accident. I'm guessing probably not, but I'm so grateful this lady did."

The doorbell then rang again. Bob and Bella hurried to answer it. This time, they found Alex and Katie, each carrying a box. Bob welcomed them, and they followed him to join Sarah and Amy.

"Our grandmother ordered us to bring you these as a thank-you for all that you have done for us," said Alex and Katie together as they handed the boxes to Sarah and Amy. Each box was filled with delicious pastries.

"They look amazing," said Sarah. "Thank you very much. Please be sure to relay a special thank-you to your grandmother for us. She is such a nice lady. How are she and your grandfather doing?"

Katie answered, "They both seem very tired. I'm worried about them. I wish I knew what I should do for them."

"Your grandparents are going to miss your mother so much. Alex and Katie, you both have to keep in touch with them at least once a week, if not more often. Those are my words of wisdom to you," said Sarah.

"And how is your dad doing?" asked Bob.

"He seems rather distracted, by what, I don't know. I guess by something at work. He did say that he may have to go on a short business trip in a day or so. He asked our grandparents if they would be able to stay with us while he is gone. Of course, they agreed."

"I didn't realize your father had to travel for business," said Bob. To tell you the truth, I don't remember him ever going on a business trip."

"It must be something new with the firm," commented Alex.

"Could be," said Bob. "I just think it is unfortunate that he should have to travel now. I think your grandparents need his presence and support."

"I agree. I think they still have many questions to ask him about the night of the accident. A couple of times, my grandfather has attempted to discuss what happened, but my dad has abruptly changed the subject. I am thinking he does not want to talk about it since he feels guilty about the argument they had. But my grandparents need to know what happened to cause the death of their only daughter. I am surprised they are as patient with my dad as they are."

"Hopefully, your dad will come to grips with what happened and be able to discuss it with you and your grandparents. It will help all of you, especially your dad," said Bob hoping to lighten the mood.

Amy offered to get something to drink for all, and her gesture was happily received. She went to the kitchen and returned with large glasses of freshly made iced tea and opened one of the boxes of pastries. The somber atmosphere soon did a turnaround. All took turns bringing up delightful episodes that had taken place in the past with the two families. Finally, it was time for Alex and Katie to leave.

Sarah told them, "Do not be strangers. Please come visit us often. Feel free to call anytime, if you need help with something."

"Thank you all. Hope to see you again soon, Amy," Alex and Katie shouted as they left.

As soon as the front door was closed, Bella began barking. Amy got the message and went in search of Bella's leash and the two of them left on a walk. Amy gone, Sarah turned to Bob, "Alex and Katie are such wonderful kids. Matt and Peggy were truly blessed. It breaks my heart to think that Peggy was a murderer. I cannot imagine what effect that information will have on Alex and Katie and their grandparents."

"I'm afraid it will have a devastating effect on them when Peggy is announced as the murderer of Ralph Benson. We will have to be there to give them extra special support," said Bob. He had no sooner said these words when Amy and Bella returned.

That was close, thought Sarah. *I really don't want Amy knowing Peggy was a murderer, although I fear I will have no choice. I wonder how she will respond. I will just have to be ready to help her understand.*

The rest of the evening was spent relaxing in the family room. Bella curled up on the couch between Sarah and Amy and looked to each of them to give her attention. She in turn gave them thank-you licks. Bob stretched out in his recliner. All settled in, they engaged in light conversation, but certain topics were decidedly off-limits. They did not talk about the Lowes or the Porters, Detective Smith, or the Calm Woods Cove Women's Club. They talked about Elizabeth. They could not wait to meet her. She looked so pretty in the photo Ryan had shown them. They were wondering what she was like. They were surprised at how serious about her Ryan sounded even though he had only known her for a few months. Is a wedding to take place soon? It was a happy thought.

Soon it was time for all to retire for the night. As she pushed herself up from the couch, Sarah looked at her husband, her daughter, and of course Bella.

I am truly blessed. As she thought that she could feel all the tension in her body drift away. She knew she was going to be able to enjoy a wonderful night's sleep so that she would be ready to face whatever was going to be coming her way the next day. But for now, she was all calm and serene.

CHAPTER 13

The End Is Near

Sarah awoke Friday feeling well-rested and cheered up after a good night of deep sleep. She was ready to face the world. She prepared a special breakfast for Bob, Amy, and herself, and all three enjoyed some special moments together until Bob had to leave for work. Amy had a 10:30 a.m. flight back to Vanderbilt to catch at Kennedy Airport so mother and daughter quickly cleaned up the kitchen and readied themselves for the trip to the airport. Just as they were about to go out the door to the garage, the phone began ringing. Sarah answered it and heard Detective Smith's voice.

"Sarah, I would like to get together with you today and clean up some loose ends. What time would be good for you?"

"I am just leaving to take Amy to Kennedy Airport, but I could meet you in your office about eleven this morning."

"Great. I'll see you then."

The traffic to Kennedy Airport was horrendous. There had been a major accident on the Cross Bronx Expressway earlier that morning, and there were still significant residual delays on both levels of the George Washington Bridge. Sarah was certain Amy was going to miss her flight. Luckily, however, the traffic eased somewhat after they crossed the bridge, and they arrived at the airport thirty minutes before the flight. Sarah hurriedly said goodbye to Amy and then prayed that her daughter would make it to the boarding gate before the plane took off.

Sarah's ride home from the airport was uneventful. In fact, she made it back to Calm Woods Cove in record time. But, because of the earlier delays, it was already 11:20 a.m. by the time Sarah pulled into the parking lot behind the Municipal Building. Detective Smith was standing waiting for her when she arrived at his office door.

"Come in, Sarah, sit down. I think we have some things to clear up. First, besides the gun, the partial remains of a letter were also found in Peggy's car. From what we were able to piece together, it appears that it was addressed to you, and it was demanding that you hire Frank Millard. There was also the statement in it that said, 'Now that I've gotten Ralph Benson out of the way.' Everything seems to point to Peggy as the murderer of Ralph Benson. I am sorry. I am going to wait until next week to present this fact to her husband and parents. I would prefer to keep this quiet in order to protect her family's good name, but my hands are tied. The police department has received much criticism lately not only from the public at large but also and most especially from Ralph Benson's family. To them, it seems that we are doing nothing to find Ralph's murderer."

"I understand your position. It just seems so unfair though that those who are going to pay for the crime, so to speak, are the innocent bystanders—Peggy's family. I especially feel sorry for Matt, Alex, and Katie. Katie read a beautiful poem about her mother at the funeral and now she will have to face the fact that not only was her mother not perfect, but she was a cold-blooded murderer."

Sarah was on the verge of tears at this point. Sensing this, Detective Smith abruptly changed the subject.

"Now that we know who killed Ralph Benson, I think you can set about hiring a new custodian for the club."

"I agree. I will talk to Laurie Johnson and make a decision today. Hopefully, the new custodian will be able to start working at the club Monday. Next Wednesday is the Annual Club luncheon and the last meeting until September, and I would feel much better knowing that we have a full-time custodian in place again."

"Okay, I will leave Joe in place at the club until you advise otherwise."

"Thank you. Even after hiring a new custodian, I may need Joe to explain things to him. By the way, I wish Joe was looking for a permanent job. He has been terrific!"

"Glad to hear it!"

"Is there anything else we have to discuss?"

"No, I guess that is all for now. Just let me know what you decide about the custodial job. I, in turn, will forewarn you when the announcement is going to be made that Peggy Lowe was the murderer of Ralph Benson."

"Have a good weekend."

"Thanks. You too."

Sarah drove directly home from the station. She was anxious now to settle the custodial situation and went right for the phone. First, she called Lillian Callan at the club office to see if there were any new candidates for the custodial job. There were none. Next, she called Laurie Johnson. She expected to have to leave a message, but surprisingly, Laurie answered the phone. Sarah explained to her that Detective Smith thought it was a good time to put a new permanent custodian into place, especially since the club year was about to end.

'So, who do you think is our best candidate, Frank Millard or Raymond Garcia?" asked Sarah.

"I would go with Frank Millard, especially in light of Peggy's untimely death."

"That is fine with me. I will give him a call immediately. Hopefully, he will be able to start Monday."

Sarah and Laurie conversed a little while longer and then agreed to meet at the club Monday morning at nine thirty so that they could greet the new custodian together.

Again, Sarah dialed the phone. Frank Millard's wife answered. Frank was not at home she told Sarah, but she would have him call her as soon as he returned. Sarah thanked her and then hung up.

I hope he calls soon. I want to get this settled once and for all, Sarah thought to herself.

By now, it was already after 1:00 p.m., and Sarah was getting very hungry for lunch. She found some odds and ends in the refrigerator and was just sitting down to enjoy them when the phone rang. It was Bob. He wanted to know if Amy had gotten off all right. Sarah told him about the traffic jam, but added that she thought that Amy should have been able to just make her flight.

Sarah returned to eating her lunch, but the phone rang again. This time it was Frank Millard. Sarah thanked him for returning her call and then explained why she had called him. Frank thanked her profusely, but then explained that he had just returned from St. Andrew's where he had been offered his old job back at a slight increase in salary to boot. He, of course, had accepted their offer. Sarah told him she was very pleased for him and his family and wished them much luck.

After hanging up the phone, Sarah just stood still for a few minutes in numb disbelief.

Looking upward, she said, "Peggy, if you only had been patient, you would not be where you are now."

Back to reality, Sarah picked up the phone and dialed Laurie Johnson's number.

"Laurie, hi. It's Sarah. You won't believe this. Frank Millard got his old job back at St. Andrew's, just this morning. I guess we have no choice but to hire Raymond Garcia. You, Penny, and I will just have to stay on the alert for any problems he might have communicating with our club members, or even more importantly, with our clients."

"I do think he can handle the work, but I am a bit worried about his lack of fluency in English. If you, Penny, and I keep on top of the situation and make him feel at ease to come to us with any questions he has, I think he will work out just fine."

"I agree. I'll give Mr. Garcia a call. If he has found a job suddenly, I think I will resign as president."

"Now, Sarah, you can't say that. You're not a quitter. Think positively. See you Monday at 9:30."

Sarah called Raymond Garcia. He answered the phone himself and was most happy to receive the good news, and yes, he would be at the clubhouse at ten Monday morning.

Thank God, that is finally settled, Sarah said to herself.

Sarah went back to finishing her lunch and then decided to go to the mall. Maybe she could find a new dress to wear to the annual luncheon Wednesday.

Two hours later, she returned home, well exercised, after having walked back and forth on both levels of the mall. It had been very relaxing looking at all the merchandise in the different stores, but she had not bought a thing. She had tried on several dresses but had nixed them all. She would just have to rely on one of her old favorites on Wednesday.

Bob returned home shortly after Sarah had. She told him about the custodial job. He was happy to hear that it was turning out that both men, after all this time, were going to be gainfully employed.

"Well, let's go celebrate their good news," Bob suggested.

"What do you have in mind?" Sarah asked.

"I thought we might go to that little Italian restaurant on Moro Street and then take in a movie."

"Sounds great. Let's go," Sarah said as she jumped up from her chair and grabbed Bob's hand.

CHAPTER 14

A Little Respite

"Can you believe it? It is Saturday already. What a week! One of our closest friends is killed in a car accident, and then we find out for certain that she was the murderer of one of the nicest men whoever was, just because he had the job she wanted her cousin's husband to have, and then when her cousin's husband can have the job, he no longer needs it. And the fact that all this has to do with the custodial position at the Calm Woods Cove Women's Club makes it even more strange. This is all too much for my feeble brain to comprehend."

"Sarah, tell you what, let's take today off from any of these problems."

"Okay, but first, I must call Detective Smith and let him know that Raymond Garcia is going to be starting in the custodial position on Monday."

Sarah made the call. Detective Smith was glad to hear that, come Monday, both Frank Millard and Raymond Garcia were going to be employed. He also promised to leave Joe at the club to help Raymond get started with his new position.

"Now, I am ready to forget all Women's Club business," Sarah told Bob. "What shall we do today?"

Bob was just about to answer Sarah's question when the phone rang. It was Bruce Langley, one of Bob's associates at work. Since the weatherman had predicted beautiful weather for Saturday and

Sunday, he and his wife, Lois, had just decided to spend the weekend on their sailboat and wanted to know if Sarah and Bob wanted to join them. After consulting with Sarah, Bob replied, "When shall we be ready?"

"How about you and Sarah meet us at our dock in Norwalk at noon."

"That sounds great."

Bob and Bruce then spent a few more minutes on the phone working out specific details.

"This is great! I truly will be able to forget all about Women's Club business for a while," Sarah exclaimed happily.

Sarah and Bob were truly excited at the prospect of spending a couple of days sailing. They had gone with Bruce and Lois several times the previous summer and thoroughly enjoyed themselves each time.

Bruce and Lois were veteran sailors, having been involved with it for over twenty-two years. In fact, they first met each other at a sailing school at City Island, New York. When they were first married, they owned a twenty-three-foot boat, and gradually, over the years, they upgraded and upsized their boat five times. Now they own a forty-six-foot Swan—a truly beautiful, stylish, and prized sailboat known for its cruising and racing abilities. They keep their boat, *Memorable Interludes* at Norwalk Cove Marina.

Sarah and Bob quickly began preparing for their weekend adventure. Since Bob had agreed to meet Bruce and Lois in Norwalk at noon, they did not have any time to waste since the trip from Calm Woods Cove to Norwalk was about a ninety-minute drive. Finally, the car was packed with all their weekend needs, and they set out on their way. They were pleased to find the traffic to be rather light and arrived at their destination ahead of schedule. Bruce and Lois, however, were already aboard their boat. They warmly welcomed Sarah and Bob and showed them to their cabin, down below with its adjoining bathroom facilities. After they had properly put away their belongings, Sarah and Bob rejoined their host and hostess up on deck for lunch.

After lunch, Bruce listened to his all-weather radio and learned that the winds were just beginning to pick up. One often experiences the doldrums around noon, and today was no exception. Luckily though, it appeared that they would have good sailing winds soon.

About 2:00 p.m., Bruce decided that it was about time for them to leave the dock. They motored out of the harbor and into Long Island Sound where the men put up the mainsail and the jib. By this time, the winds had indeed picked up, and soon, they were cruising at a speed of six knots.

Sarah could feel herself escaping into a whole new world as they sailed back and forth across the sound between Connecticut and Long Island. She just loved the feel of the wind blowing through her hair and the smell of saltwater. It was so invigorating!

The two couples enjoyed sailing all afternoon. The winds were perfect and offered all an ideal sailing experience. About 6:00 p.m., they headed back into the harbor and then to the Langley's dock. After they had fastened the boat securely for the night, they all cleaned up for dinner and then walked to a local waterfront restaurant well-known for its delicious seafood. They were shown to a table overlooking the harbor and presented with menus listing a host of incredible sounding selections. Sarah and Bob chose lobster dishes while Lois and Bruce chose shrimp and sea bass. They ended their meals with a fresh strawberry shortcake and coffee.

Feeling wonderfully satiated, they casually walked back along the docks looking at all the boats until they decided to call it a night and headed back to *Memorable Interludes* for a refreshing night's sleep on the water. While Sarah and Bob were relaxing in their cabin, they could hear fish jumping in the waters around the boat.

"I just love being here. It is so peaceful. Nothing like returning to nature to help renew your spirits," Sarah exclaimed.

"You are so right. I am really grateful to Bruce and Lois for having invited us this weekend. It was just what you needed. I had been trying to think of what I could do to cheer you up after the terrible week you have been through, but I really had not come up with an answer. Thank you, Bruce and Lois, from both of us."

Sarah and Bob fell gradually to sleep in each other's arms and slept soundly, while the boat swayed gently back and forth with the rolling of the waters beneath it.

CHAPTER 15

The Escape Continues

Sarah and Bob were awakened about 8:00 a.m. by a flurry of activity in the waters around them. Many of the nearby boaters were heading out to sail, fish, or to just take advantage of the beautiful early morning weather. Sarah and Bob stirred from their cabin and found Lois and Bruce up on deck.

"Come on up and join us for some coffee," Lois called to them.

Sarah and Bob settled themselves on the deck, while Bruce gave them the daily weather report.

"They are promising us a perfect day. The sun should continue to shine brightly, and the winds are supposed to be a sailor's dream all afternoon long."

The two couples finished their coffee and then dressed for church. They attended a service at St. Bridget's Church, which was about a fifteen-minute ride from the marina. After church, they enjoyed a wonderful brunch at a small diner near the church and then returned to the boat to enjoy an afternoon of sailing.

On Saturday, only Bruce and Bob had actually manned the boat. Sarah and Lois had just enjoyed the benefits of their husbands' expert sailing abilities. Today, however, the men decided that the women should not just be passengers, but that they should, from time to time, help as crew, so that the men could relax and take in the scenery for a while.

This proved to be quite interesting. Lois was an excellent sailor and really could almost handle the boat by herself. Sarah, however, was a complete novice. Even though she and Bob had sailed with the Langleys before, Sarah had never done any of the actual "sailing." She had never even been at the helm. When she first took over the wheel, she had difficulty staying on course, and at one point, she was steering the boat around in a circle. Even Sarah had to laugh at this. She also found it difficult to keep the sails in optimal trim. As a result, they began to flap, or according to sail terms, "luff." Gradually, however, she got the hang of it. In fact, by the end of the day, she received high praise from Bruce for the way she had maneuvered the boat around the hundreds of lobster pots in the sound.

"Many a sailor has caused great damage to his boat by getting caught on one of those pots," Bruce had warned.

By midafternoon, all were looking for some refreshments, so since he was at the helm, Bruce decided to show Sarah and Bob one of his favorite anchorage spots. It was the cove at Lloyd Harbor. The cove was created decades ago by sand mining when the area belonged to the department store magnate, Marshall Field, and the industrialist, S. E. Fairchild. Field's 1,500-acre estate became Caumsett State Park, whose name, aptly enough, comes from the Matinecock Indian term for Lloyd Neck, "the place by the sharp rock."

Bruce explained, "The cove has been a popular destination for boaters for years. It is sheltered by a spit of land from the north and the jetty from the south. But the channel has been filling in with tide-driven sand for years, to the point that it is now just twenty-five feet wide and less than two feet deep at low tide, shallow enough to ground nearly anything bigger than a rowboat. And the jagged rocks at the tip of the jetty are now underwater so at high tide, they are lying in wait to gore a wayward hull."

Bruce gingerly navigated the narrow channel boaters call Clam Diggers Cove and residents call the Sand Hole. As they entered the basin, they enjoyed looking at the multitude of birds on the surrounding lands. Bruce explained to them that no humans were allowed on the land "because the area is a bird sanctuary and a very sensitive area," he said. "There is a huge migration of turtles and crabs that hatch and go out into the sound."

Once inside the cove, Bruce selected a spot, a fair distance away from three other boats, and dropped anchor. The two couples enjoyed sandwiches, cookies, and soft drinks along with a feeling of peace and relaxation provided by the scenery.

"We love to anchor here at least three or four times during a summer," Lois said. "It is a great anchorage and usually doesn't get too crowded. Also, if you like swimming in the sound, this is probably one of the best places to do so."

The time passed quickly, and before they knew it, it was already 4:00 p.m. It was time to lift anchor and sail again. Once back out on the sound, they found that the wind had shifted and had picked up speed. *Memorable Interludes* was soon skimming across the water at more than nine knots. The boat was also heeling a great deal causing all passengers to be sprayed with cool saltwater.

On the way back, Bruce pointed out the US Coast Guard Station at Eton's Neck and gave Sarah and Bob a mini history lesson.

"George Washington was the one that signed the original order to have the station built at Eton's Neck way back in 1792. And the Eton Neck's station is reportedly today considered to be the fourth busiest station in the US, ranking behind only Miami, Cape May, New Jersey, and San Francisco."

He added, "I know I believe it. There are certainly enough boats on the sound on any given summer weekend to greatly increase the odds of the Coast Guard's services being needed."

Making a surprise change in topic, Bruce turned to Sarah and asked, "How about taking the helm?"

"I don't think that would be a good idea," Sarah replied. "It is far too windy now. I had enough trouble when the winds were calmer."

"Okay, I'll let you off this time. Did you note I said this time?"

"Oh yes."

Even though Sarah was reluctant to take the helm, Bob jumped at the chance. He truly loved being at the helm, especially when the sailboat was gliding swiftly through the water.

They arrived back at the dock at 7:00 p.m. It was just getting dark. An hour was then spent closing the boat and packing up everyone's belongings. By this time, there were four very hungry and tired people. They decided to go to Margo's Restaurant at the marina where they were served copious amounts of food. After dinner, Sarah and Bob thanked Bruce and Lois profusely for the wonderful weekend and said goodbye. The two couples then headed separately back to New Jersey.

"Now that was a great weekend," Bob exclaimed.

"It sure was, and I learned something very special during it," Sarah responded.

"And what was that?"

"I learned that my husband is a great sailor."

"Do you really think so?"

"Of course. I wouldn't say it if I didn't. I just have one question for you. Are you thinking we should get our own boat?"

"Not a bad idea. What do you think?"

"I think I had better learn a lot more about sailing before we do a thing like that."

CHAPTER 16

Reality Strikes

Monday morning. It had come far too quickly for Sarah and Bob. In their minds, they were still on the Langleys' boat cruising across Long Island Sound. They both knew they had to get it up and out of bed, but that was going to be very difficult to do today. Neither one was anxious to face the responsibilities awaiting them. Bob was scheduled to meet with a potentially challenging foreign client. And of course, Sarah was to meet with Raymond Garcia and officially hire him as the new custodian of the Calm Woods Cove Women's Club. She was not looking forward to going to the clubhouse. In fact, she felt quite nervous about it, since every time she had been there lately something awful happened. But then she reminded yourself, *Peggy was the cause of those happenings. She is dead. She could not possibly harm anyone now.*

Sarah was the first one to bravely climb out of bed. She put on her bathrobe and slippers and went downstairs to begin fixing breakfast. Bob came down dressed for work, about thirty minutes later. They each enjoyed a bagel with cream cheese and cherry preserves, a glass of orange juice, and coffee. After breakfast, Bob left for work as he wished Sarah good luck with Raymond Garcia. Sarah wished Bob good luck with his client.

Sarah quickly cleaned up the kitchen and then went upstairs to shower and dress. While in the shower, she felt as if everything were rocking, as if she were still onboard *Memorable Interludes*. She had never experienced this phenomenon before, but she had heard others describing this happening to them. She was almost, in fact, beginning to feel a little seasick.

Now this is ridiculous. I am not even on the boat. How could I possibly feel seasick?

But she did, so she ended her shower, dried herself off, put on her robe, and went to lie down on her bed for a while. Before she knew it, she had fallen sound asleep. Luckily, forty minutes into her sleep, the phone rang and awakened her. She put her hand out and picked up the receiver.

"Hello."

"Hello, Sarah, it's Lillian Callan. I am calling to tell you that I will not be at the clubhouse today. I've been sick all night with a stomach virus. Hopefully, it is just a twenty-four-hour bug and I will be able to make it to the office tomorrow."

"Lillian, don't worry about the office. I do hope you feel better quickly. Laurie Johnson and I are going to be meeting with Raymond Garcia this morning, so since I will be at the clubhouse anyway. I'll take care of any pressing matters while I am there."

"Thanks, Sarah. I appreciate that."

"Now take care of yourself. I'll talk to you soon."

After hanging up the phone, Sarah looked at the clock on her nightstand. It was already 9:00 a.m.

I can't believe I fell back to sleep. Thank heavens Lillian called.

Sarah got up off the bed and was happy to find that she no longer felt seasick. She dressed quickly, did her hair, tidied up the bedroom, and then left for the club.

She pulled into the clubhouse parking lot at the same time as Laurie Johnson. After parking their cars, the two women walked to the kitchen door of the clubhouse together. Sarah unlocked the door and then once she and Laurie were inside, she relocked it. Ever since the shattering mirror incident, all clubhouse doors to the outside were being kept locked at all times.

The two women then proceeded to the first-floor office. That door was also locked, so Sarah had to again use her key. Once inside the office, they checked their mailboxes. They each had a pile of letters and papers. While they were sorting through all their mail, Sarah began telling Laurie all about her great weekend. She was just getting to Sunday's events when the doorbell rang. Sarah glanced up at the office clock. It was 9:55 a.m.

"I bet that's Raymond Garcia. Let's greet him together," said Sarah.

It was, in fact, Raymond Garcia. Sarah and Laurie each shook hands hello with him and then showed him into the office. They reviewed the duties of the custodial position and asked if he had any questions. He did have a few, which they immediately answered for him.

"I think the next item on the agenda, Raymond, is to take you upstairs to meet our rental manager Penny Shriver. She will go over the events scheduled for this month, and what is required for them."

Sarah and Laurie followed by Raymond Garcia made their way upstairs to Penny Shriver's office. Sarah had not been in the office since the evening when she found Ralph Benson's body. She could feel a wave of panic welling up inside her. Thank goodness Laurie and Raymond were with her or she probably would have turned around and run home. Instead, she made it to the top of the stairs and stopped dead outside the office door. She felt like she could not move an inch further. Finally, Laurie recognized that Sarah was having a problem and she stepped ahead of her and knocked on the office door.

"Come in," Penny responded.

Laurie told Sarah to go ahead, but Sarah did not move.

"You go first, Laurie, and if all is well, I will follow."

Laurie entered the room and found Penny sitting at the desk just finishing a telephone conversation with a prospective rental client.

"Everything is fine, Sarah. You and Raymond can come in now."

They did just that and then Sarah and Laurie introduced Raymond to Penny.

"Raymond, we will leave you in Penny's hands for a while, so she can go over the schedule of events with you. After you are finished here, come back to the downstairs office."

Just as Sarah and Laurie were about to leave the room, there was a knock on the door. Penny called out to the person. "Come in."

It was Matt Lowe.

"Matt, what a surprise. What can we do for you?" Sarah asked.

With that, Matt took out a gun and aimed it at Sarah and told everyone not to move.

"Introduce me to your friends, Sarah," he said with a bitter tone in his voice.

Sarah was petrified, but she did as he asked. In a barely audible voice, she introduced the others in the room. She started with Penny and Laurie and finally Raymond using only their first names.

"Sarah, who's Raymond?"

Sarah could not find her voice to speak.

"Come on, Sarah. Tell me who Raymond is or I will be forced to kill him right now."

"Raymond is the club's new custodian," Sarah feebly answered.

"New custodian, hey. When did you make the decision to hire him? My poor wife who had devoted hours of service to the Women's Club is barely in the ground, and you betray her. You ignored her pleas on behalf of her cousin's husband while she was still alive and as soon as she is not watching you anymore, you insult her by giving the job to this Raymond. I am glad I ran into Jim Callan at the train station this morning. He told me you were planning to hire this person." He pointed to Raymond. "I am here to change your mind. You will hire Frank Millard as a special tribute to Peggy."

At this point, Sarah attempted to explain that Frank Millard was not going to be the new custodian only because he had his old job back at the church—a fact Matt evidently did not know—but as soon as she started to speak Matt told her to shut up.

"You know, Sarah, life would've been so simple if you had just hired Frank Millard instead of Ralph Benson. Peggy had told me that she thought you were going to do that. I counted on that and then you didn't. What could I do? I was forced to try to scare you into seeing the error of your decision. But you do not scare easily. What will it take to convince you to give Frank Millard the job?"

Sarah started speaking again, and this time, Matt let her. She decided that she would just play along with him.

"Matt, Frank can have the job. Let Laurie, Penny, and Raymond leave, and I will call Frank and tell him that he has the job."

"Sarah, I don't believe you. You are just saying that because I have a gun and you want to trick me into letting your friends go. No way. Call him right now, while your friends are here."

"No, let them go first."

Matt then shot a hole in the wall.

"Do I make myself clear, Sarah? Call Frank right now and depending on how the call goes, I'll decide what I'm going to do with you and your friends."

"Do you know his number?" Sarah asked Matt.

"No, I can't remember it. Call information, and no funny stuff."

Sarah got the number and then dialed it. The answering machine came on.

Sarah hung up.

"Okay, call the number back and leave a message for Frank. Tell him to call Sarah Peterson at the Calm Woods Cove Women's Club. Leave the number of the phone in this office."

Sarah did as she had been told.

"Well, folks, why don't you all sit down on the floor over there, and we will wait for Frank to call back."

"Matt, I'll stay here, but please let the others go," Sarah begged.

"No way, Sarah. This time you're not going to get your way. I want them all to hear you hiring Frank so that you won't be able to renege on the deal."

"Matt, why is it so important to you that Frank have the job?" Sarah asked.

Surprisingly, Matt answered her.

"I have debts, Sarah—lots and lots of gambling debts. I owe some dangerous people. I can't give any more money to Frank and Janice. I don't have it to give. Peggy knew that money had been tight for us, but she didn't know about my gambling debts until the night of her death. She innocently asked me if we could increase the amount we were lending Frank and Janice, and I lost my cool.

I explained what had been going on with me. And how I had tried to stack the deck at the Women's Club by killing Ralph Benson so Frank would get the job. At first, she didn't believe me, but then I showed her my gun. She was very upset and ran out of the house with it and jumped into the car. I presume she was heading to her parents' house for help when she crashed."

"You know, Matt, the police think Peggy killed Ralph Benson."

"You must be joking. Why would they think that?"

"She had been acting very strangely lately, and they found the gun and an incriminating note in her car."

"Oh, she took the note too. I didn't know that."

"What was the note?"

"I thought of committing suicide to solve my problems and had written a note explaining some things."

Just then the phone rang.

"Okay, Sarah, you are on. Do a good job of hiring."

"Hello, Calm Woods Cove Women's Club, Sarah Peterson speaking."

It was a client looking for Penny, but Matt would not let her speak, so Sarah just took a message for her.

Sarah was just about to ask Matt another question so that she could be sure that Peggy really had not been involved with the murder of Ralph Benson, but the phone rang. Again, it was a prospective client, and again, Matt would not let Penny speak.

"By the way, Matt, how did you get into the building?" Sarah asked.

"I have Peggy's keys. I have had them ever since I took them out of her purse the night I shot the mirror in the downstairs office. I would have loved to have seen your face, Sarah, after I did that, but I couldn't stay around and take the chance of being caught."

"Suppose Frank is out of town. Suppose there is no way he can get my message. How long are we going to stay here?"

"Just relax. I am sure he is not out of town. He'll be calling soon. I am sure."

With that, the phone rang again, and Sarah answered it. This time, it was Frank.

"Frank, this is Sarah Peterson. I was calling to offer you the custodial job at the Women's Club."

Sarah paused while he answered and then said, "That's great. Can you start tomorrow? Fine. we'll meet at the clubhouse say ten tomorrow morning. Goodbye."

"Not bad, Sarah. You finally came through."

"Can we leave now?"

"You can't be serious. You all know too much now. The way I look at it, I have two choices—to either kill all of you or I kill myself. Frankly, I am feeling pretty good right now and don't really feature dying quite yet."

"You plan on killing all of us?"

"Do you have another idea?"

No one answered.

"All of you stand up and face the wall. I don't want to see your faces as you die."

Sarah, Laurie, Penny, and Raymond did it as they were told. As soon as they were in place, Matt aimed the gun at the ceiling above them and shot the gun once just to scare them.

"Are you all ready? Who wants to die first?" he asked and started to laugh.

Just then, the office door opened, and Joe Finnegan burst in. He tackled Matt and forced him to drop his gun, but not before another shot rang out. The bullet hit Penny in the leg. Matt and Joe wrestled with each other for several minutes until suddenly Matt got free and ran out of the room. Joe and Raymond ran after him across the balcony, down the backstairs, and they were heading to the kitchen when they caught up with Matt who had been apprehended by Detective Smith. He was being handcuffed and read his Miranda rights.

Sarah came down to see what had happened and to wait for the ambulance she had called for Penny.

"And I am glad to see you," she said to Detective Smith. "Joe Finnegan was fantastic!"

"How did you happen to show up when you did?" Raymond asked Detective Smith.

"Ask Sarah. I'll let her tell you."

Sarah explained to Raymond and Matt who was still present.

"When the last phone call came, it was really Joe calling from the downstairs office. I hoped he would know something was wrong when I carried on such a strange conversation with him. Luckily, he did, and he called Detective Smith before coming upstairs to save us."

As Sarah finished, Matt just glowered at her

"You mean you win again Sarah. Frank still doesn't have the job?"

"Frank doesn't have the job here, but he does have a job," Sarah answered. "I tried to tell you that upstairs, but you didn't want to hear about it. He started today in his old job at the church. He even got a small raise. You did all this for nothing."

As he was leaving Matt turned to Sarah, "I am sorry, Sarah, for putting you through so much, but you can never understand the pressures I have been under as a result of my gambling. Please look after Alex and Katie for me."

"I will be glad to do that," Sarah responded.

Just as Matt was taken out of the building, the ambulance arrived for Penny. She was in great pain and had lost quite a bit of blood. One of the attendants examined her wound. It was determined that the bullet was still in her right leg, in the thigh area, but the attendant did not think it would be too difficult to remove it. He also did not believe that Penny would have any permanent damage to her leg. After the diagnosis was given, Penny was quickly whisked off to the hospital. Laurie followed the ambulance in her own car so that she could lend Penny some moral support at the hospital. That left Sarah at the clubhouse with Detective Smith, Joe Finnegan, and Raymond Garcia.

"You men are all my heroes. I hate to think what would've happened, Joe, if you had not shown up here when you did. By the way, why were you calling the rental office number?"

"I arrived at the clubhouse and saw five cars in the parking lot. No one was around downstairs so I guessed that you all must be upstairs. I was just calling to find out if you wanted me to stay around for any reason."

"Thank God you did. I really think that Matt would've killed us all, if you had not appeared on the scene. Thank you! Thank you! Thank you!"

"I am glad I was able to help."

"And I am glad that we never let on that we thought Peggy Lowe was our killer," Detective Smith said.

"I am really glad that Peggy was not a murderer," Sarah added. "It is awful that Matt was, but I can deal with that more easily. Peggy and I have been such close friends for ten years. We were almost like sisters. I had always felt that I really knew and understood her. When it seemed that she was a cold-blooded killer, I felt stupid, betrayed, and totally lacking in judgment."

"It is terrible what a devastating effect one's gambling can have on the people around him or her. Matt sacrificed everything in his life in order to focus in on his gambling and gambling debts. He is a very sick man," commented Detective Smith.

"Yes, he is, and I hope his children can understand this and forgive him for all that he has done. It'll be very difficult for them," Sarah added.

"Well, I guess the Calm Woods Cove Women's Club can get back to normal now," Joe Finnegan interjected.

"Yes," Sarah replied. "Another reason why I'm so glad Peggy was not a murderer has to do with the Women's Club. Peggy had been such a wonderful member I think if she had been guilty, it would have had a very damaging effect on the club. The way things have turned out, I believe that the club members will be able to move on now. Speaking of moving on, I think it is time, Raymond, that you get started in your new job."

"I'll be happy to get him started," Joe Finnegan spoke up.

"Thanks, Joe. That would be great."

"As soon as you are able, I would appreciate it if each of you would come down to headquarters to give your statements regarding today's happenings," Detective Smith said. "In the meantime, I will leave you all to do whatever you have to do here. See you later."

Joe and Raymond retreated to the kitchen while Sarah went to the first-floor office.

The first thing she did when she got there was to eat her lunch. Suddenly she was starving. She felt the most relaxed she had in weeks.

CHAPTER 17

The Truth

Sarah stayed at the clubhouse for an hour sorting through mail. It felt so good being able to perform her presidential duties without any fears hanging over her head. Once she had finished her tasks, she said goodbye to Joe and Raymond. It was decided that Joe would hang around for a couple more days to make sure Raymond fully understood all the duties of his job and to show him where everything was kept.

On her way home, Sarah made two stops. First, she went to the hospital to check on Penny. When she got there, she was informed that Penny was still in the recovery room after having had the bullet surgically removed, and Sarah was advised to come back during evening visiting hours. Next, Sarah went to police headquarters. As she pulled into the parking lot, she was faced with the sight of what seemed like hundreds of media people and their vehicles. She wasn't sure what she should do since all these people were here, but she decided to look for a parking space and then call Detective Smith on her cell phone and ask him.

Sarah drove around and around and up and down each lane of the parking lot and finally found a space at the farthest end of the building. She dialed Detective Smith's number. A patrolman answered. Sarah explained to him who she was and why she was calling. He told her to hold while he went to get Detective Smith. Finally, after about ten minutes Detective Smith came on the line.

"Sarah, where are you?"

"I'm in your parking lot, and I'm not sure what I should do with all the media people here."

"There's to be a press conference at 5:00 p.m. That's the reason for the circus out there. I want to talk with you, so I'll sneak out and meet you in your car. Where are you parked?"

Sarah gave him directions to her car and then waited for him to arrive. He was there within five minutes.

"Things are so hectic inside and outside around here. Somehow the word got out that someone had been arrested in the murder of Ralph Benson. Since then, there has been a media frenzy. Captain Blanchard decided that the only way to quell it and to stop any rumors was to hold a press conference."

"Is Captain Blanchard going to announce the arrest of Matt Lowe?"

"No, he is just going to say that a suspect is in custody since we have not yet talked with the Lowe children or Peggy's parents. And that is why I wanted to talk with you. Will you and your husband please accompany me when I go to tell them the facts this evening? I think they are going to need you for support."

"What you have to tell them is so awful that I would rather not be present, but you are right, they will need someone to give them support. Bob and I will accompany you."

"Thank you. I will call you at home to let you know when things have quieted down here so that I can leave to meet you at the Lowes' house."

"Fine. Bob and I will await your call."

Detective Smith got out of the car and hurried back into police headquarters. As soon as he had left, Sarah started her car and drove home.

It was almost 5:00 p.m. when Sarah got inside the house. She turned on the television and waited for the news to come on. At exactly the moment the new antique clock on her family room mantelpiece chimed 5 o'clock, the reporter on Channel 4 began.

"Our top story for today, Monday, June 7—Police have finally made an arrest in the killing of Ralph Benson. The identity of the suspect has not been revealed yet, but police are hoping to disclose more details soon pending notification of persons connected with the case. Let us go live now to police headquarters and Captain David Blanchard."

The camera zoomed in on Captain Blanchard who was standing on the front steps of police headquarters with Detective Smith. He recounted the history of Ralph Benson's murder and then announced that a suspect was indeed in custody, but that the identity of the suspect could not be revealed at the present time. He then asked if there were any questions. Of course, the reporters immediately hurled a barrage of questions at him. He deftly fielded them all without really telling them any more than they already knew. After about ten minutes, Captain Blanchard and Detective Smith thanked the crowd of reporters and retreated inside the building.

Just as the news conference ended, the phone rang. It was Bob.

"Sarah, I just heard the report that a suspect has been arrested in Ralph Benson's murder. Is that true? Have they really come up with someone other than Peggy?"

"Yes, that's the good part. I would rather tell you the whole story when you get home."

Suddenly, Sarah felt overwhelmed by fatigue and dread. She really was not looking forward to going to the Lowes'. She decided to take a nice long shower, put on some fresh clothes, and lay down on her bed in the hope of reviving herself. She fell asleep for about twenty minutes and awoke, feeling a bit better. She got up and went down to the kitchen to fix dinner and await Bob's arrival. He pulled into the garage at 6:20 p.m.

Bob poured a glass of wine for each of them and then they sat at the kitchen table, while Sarah went over the day's events. Bob was astounded. He was also visibly very upset when he learned of Matt's arrest for the murder of Ralph Benson.

"Now I understand why you said earlier on the phone, 'that's the good part,' when I asked if they had really come up with a suspect other than Peggy for the murder of Ralph Benson."

"Has Matt ever mentioned his gambling to you?"

"One time, he mentioned that he had gone by bus to Atlantic City with some group—I don't remember what group—and that he had won $1,000 playing the slot machines. He said I should join him the next time he goes. But he never said anything about it again."

"Oh, by the way, Detective Smith wants us to go with him tonight when he tells Alex, Katie, and Peggy's parents about Matt's arrest. I gather they suspect nothing. They think Matt is on a business trip."

"This is going to be very difficult."

"Yes, I agree. If my conscience would let me, I would tell Detective Smith to leave me out of this, but I know in my heart I should be there when he tells them."

Just then the phone rang. It was Detective Smith.

"Can you meet me in an hour at the Lowes'?" he asked.

"Yes, that will be fine," Sarah responded.

Sarah told Bob the game plan and then served dinner. During dinner, Bob told Sarah all about his meeting with the foreign client.

"Three other fellows in our office had tried to work with him but gave up. I was chosen as the next candidate to give it a whirl. Well, even if I do say so myself, things went very well between us. He and I appear to be on the same wavelength. I am quite sure we will be able to work together."

"Congratulations! I'm glad to hear something went well today."

Sarah cleaned up after dinner and then it was time for them to go to the Lowes'.

Sarah and Bob reached the Lowes' and pulled in behind Detective Smith's car which was parked in the driveway. As they got out of their car, Detective Smith got out of his. He told them that their timing was perfect for he had just pulled into the driveway a minute ahead of them.

Sarah and Bob walked to the front door with Detective Smith leading the way. Sarah truly felt like turning around and running away, but of course, she didn't.

Detective Smith rang the doorbell and the three of them waited with hearts beating nervously for someone to answer it. Several minutes went by. Detective Smith rang the bell again and again. They waited.

"I can't believe no one is home. I called them earlier to tell them we were coming over. This is very strange. I'll go back to my car and try their phone number," Detective Smith said.

Sarah and Bob rang the bell again and waited. Still, no one came.

Detective Smith called to them, "It appears that no one is home. They are not answering their phone either. I really don't understand this. I'm going to walk around the house to see if I detect any foul play. You two stay here."

After about ten minutes, Detective Smith returned to their point of vision.

"Nothing seems to be amiss on the outside. Do you know what kind of car or cars they could be driving?"

Sarah gave Detective Smith a description of the Lowes' remaining car since Peggy's accident and then asked what he planned to do.

"I'm going to put out an APB on the two Lowe children, Peggy's parents, and the car. Hopefully, they will turn up soon. In the meantime, you go home, and I will contact you as soon as I learn anything."

Sarah and Bob climbed into their car and drove home.

"I do not feel good about this at all," Sarah said. "Something is very wrong. I wish there was something we could do. I just hate sitting around waiting."

"I feel the same way. I guess we could call around and see if anyone has seen them."

Sarah was on her fifth call. So far no one had seen nor spoken that day with anyone at the Lowe house. Suddenly, the call waiting feature on her phone beeped in. She quickly ended her present conversation and took the incoming call.

It was Detective Smith.

"We found Alex, Katie, and Mr. and Mrs. Porter. They are at the hospital. Ed Porter had severe chest pains, so his wife and grandchildren drove him to the emergency room."

"Oh. I can't believe this. I am going to tell Bob, and then he and I will head off to the hospital. If you need us, you can reach us there, and don't worry, I don't intend to discuss Matt with them."

"We will have to, but now is definitely not the time."

"I don't know if there ever will be a good time, the way things have been going with the Lowes lately."

"Well, hopefully, Mr. Porter will stabilize soon, and we will be able to tell Alex and Katie about their father. Captain Blanchard won't be able to keep a lid on the name of Ralph Benson's murderer too much longer. The pressure from the media is awful, and there is always the risk that someone on the inside will spill the beans."

Sarah hung up the phone and then she and Bob hurried to the hospital. They went to the emergency room entrance. In the waiting room down the hallway, they found Alex and Katie. Alex was trying to comfort his sister who was crying. They were both very glad to see Sarah and Bob.

After saying a few words in an effort to comfort the Lowe children, Sarah inquired as to what had happened.

Alex responded, "About 7:30 p.m., the doorbell rang. Our grandfather went to answer it thinking it was you and Detective Smith. Instead, there were two rather large tough-looking guys who asked for my dad. When my grandfather told them he wasn't at home, they proceeded to launch into a threatening speech. They said that Dad owed thousands of dollars for gambling debts and that he had better pay off within twenty-four hours or all hell would break loose. One of the guys then put his hand on my grandfather's shoulder, shook him a bit, and said, 'Gramps, make sure he gets this message.' The two men then left. As my grandfather was closing the door, he started to sweat and complained of pains in his chest, so we immediately brought him here. We are waiting for the doctor to give us input on his condition. My grandmother is with him."

"How is your grandmother doing?" Bob asked.

"She is trying to remain strong, but I can tell she's on the verge of breaking down. I don't know if she can take much more," Katie replied. "It was enough losing my mother, her daughter, now if something happens to her husband too…" Then Katie began to cry.

"She is lucky she has both of you. You've got to help keep her spirits up. Promise me you will do that, and I will try to keep yours up," Sarah said comfortingly.

Dr. Vincent Carrillo entered the waiting room. He was the top cardiac specialist in the area and luckily associated with the hospital. He walked over to Alex and Katie to give them an update on their grandfather.

"Your grandfather is resting comfortably now. We believe his symptoms were caused by atrial fibrillation—AFib—which is a quivering or irregular heartbeat known medically as arrhythmia. The term *arrhythmia* refers to any change from the normal sequence of electrical impulses causing the heart to beat too fast, too slowly, or erratically. When the heart doesn't beat properly, it can't pump blood effectively. When the heart doesn't pump blood effectively, the lungs, brain, and all other organs can't work properly and may shut down or be damaged."

"What effect has this had on my grandfather?" asked Alex looking frightened by all these medical facts.

"We did a standard, noninvasive echocardiogram. A technician spread gel on your grandfather's chest and then pressed a device known as a transducer firmly against his skin, aiming an ultrasound beam through his chest to his heart. The transducer recorded the sound wave echoes from his heart. A computer converted the echoes into moving images on a monitor of his heart's chambers, valves, walls, and the blood vessels—aorta, arteries, veins—attached to his heart. The procedure took about thirty minutes. The good news is that your grandfather's heart appears to be very healthy. We believe that his symptoms were caused by the terribly stressful incident he endured. It caused his heart to beat erratically. Luckily, his heart was able to correct itself. To make sure that his heartbeat is stable, we are going to attach a Holter monitor to him which will record twenty-four hours of continuous electrocardiographic signals. If no signs of arrhythmia are detected, we will release him. We are moving your grandfather to room 205, and once he is settled in, we will attach the Holter monitor.

Alex and Katie both thanked Dr. Carrillo and then he gave them an assignment.

"I would like you to take your grandmother home for some rest. I told her to go home, but she argued with me that she is afraid she won't be informed of any changes. You can tell her that Dr. Carrillo has instructed one of the nurses that once she does go home to let her know immediately of any significant changes."

"Thank you for doing that. I think that should assuage her fears. Now, Katie and I will work on making sure she gets some rest."

"Good. I knew I could count on both of you. I will check on your grandfather in the morning, and of course, I will be on call all night," Dr. Carrillo said as he bid them goodnight and exited the room.

After Dr. Carrillo left, Alex and Katie began talking about how to persuade their grandmother to go home to get some rest.

"I have an idea," Bob said. "Sarah and I will take her home with us. You two can stay here and keep us informed."

"Thank you! That is a great idea. I hope we can talk her into it. I am going to go talk to her now," Katie said.

Ten minutes or so later, Monica Porter walked into the waiting room. She really looked exhausted.

"I hear you have been nice enough to offer to take me home with you to take a nap?"

"Yes, and anytime you want to come back to the hospital, I'll be happy to bring you," Bob said.

Once home, Sarah and Bob offered Monica something to eat or drink, but she turned them down. She was too tired, so Sarah showed her to the guest room. After their guest was settled in, Sarah and Bob noticed that their answering machine light was blinking. There was only one message on it. It was from Detective Smith.

"Sarah and Bob, please give me a call at the station as soon as you can."

Bob called the station, and Detective Smith picked up.

"How is Mr. Porter doing?"

"He has stabilized."

"Did anyone happen to say what might have precipitated his chest pains?"

"Yes, I almost forgot. You do not know the story."

Bob then detailed for Detective Smith the happenings at the Lowes' house earlier in the evening. He finished by saying, "Dr. Carrillo believes that the visit from the two thugs caused Ed Porter's heart to go into AFIB. It has now stabilized, but as a precaution, they are monitoring him for the next twenty-four hours."

"It sounds like he is going to be okay. How is his wife taking all this?"

"It has been very hard on her. But since her husband seemed to be doing well, at the doctor's suggestion, we just brought Monica here so that she can get some rest."

"This case gets more complicated all the time. For everyone's safety, I don't want anyone to go back to the Lowes' house. In the meantime, I'm going to do some investigating into what happened there. Call me if there are any changes in Mr. Porter's condition."

"I will."

Sarah and Bob were now thoroughly exhausted themselves and turned in for the night.

CHAPTER 18

A Slow Return to Calm

Sarah and Bob were awakened the next morning at six by a knocking at their bedroom door. Sarah got out of bed, put on a robe, and opened the door. Monica Porter was standing there with an anxious look on her face.

"I have been awake since four thirty, but I thought that was much too early an hour to awaken you. It is 6:00 a.m. now, and I was wondering if I could impose upon you to take me back to the hospital. I really do want to be back there with my husband."

"Of course, I quite understand. Let me find something for you for breakfast, and while you eat, I will get dressed," responded Sarah.

Forty minutes later, the two women were back at the hospital. They found Katie just as she was waking up from a short nap on a couch in the waiting room.

"Where is Alex?" Monica asked.

"He is with grandpa," Katie answered.

"Let's go find him," said Sarah.

Monica, Katie, and Sarah headed to Ed Porter's room. They found Alex sitting by his grandfather's bed, and the two males were engaged in lively conversation. Everyone was so happy to see that Ed was definitely feeling much better.

All visited with Ed for a few minutes, and then Dr. Carrillo came on the scene. He asked everyone to step out in the hall for a few minutes, while he did a brief checkup of his patient. While waiting for Dr. Carrillo, Sarah told Alex and Katie that Detective Smith did not want them going to their house until he gave his okay. She explained that he was doing an investigation into the men who had put their grandfather in the hospital.

"Alex and Katie, you are most welcome at my house. Why don't you come back with me now for some breakfast, a shower, a nap, whatever?" said Sarah.

Katie decided that since she had just awakened from a nap, she would stay at the hospital and grab something to eat in the cafeteria. Alex, however, said he would be grateful to Sarah for some breakfast and the use of a bed.

Shortly after this was decided, a nurse came out to get them and said Dr. Carrillo wanted to talk to them inside by his patient. They went back into room 205 and joined Dr. Carrillo and Ed.

"I'm happy to tell you that my patient is coming along well. The monitor has shown no new episodes of arrhythmia. If all remains stable, Ed, you can go home tomorrow morning."

Everyone, of course, was greatly cheered by this news. Sarah and Alex told Ed that they would be back later to see him and then left for Sarah's house.

Sarah arrived home just as Bob was beginning to prepare himself some breakfast. She gave him the latest update on Ed and then explained that Alex would be joining them for breakfast.

After breakfast, Bob left for work, and Alex went to take a nap. Sarah was just finishing cleaning up the kitchen when the phone rang. It was Detective Smith.

"How is Ed Porter?"

Sarah updated him.

"Sarah, I have some very interesting information to tell you. Can you come to my office at noon?" asked Detective Smith.

"Certainly. I shall see you then," responded Sarah.

I wonder what he has to tell me, she mused to herself. *He certainly has my curiosity aroused!*

Alex awoke around 10:00 a.m., thanked Sarah for her hospitality, and left for the hospital. Sarah then left for the Women's Club.

She wanted to make sure everything was being readied for the annual meeting and lunch the next day. When she arrived at the clubhouse, she found Raymond and Joe busily setting up the tables and chairs in the ballroom. She greeted them and then asked how everything was going. She was happy to hear that all was quiet and that a large turnout was expected for the luncheon the next day.

Sarah left them to finish their work and headed for the first-floor office. Lillian Callan was sitting behind her desk, but she looked wiped out.

"Lillian, how are you feeling?" Sarah greeted her.

"Better, just tired, but Penny isn't here today. She probably has the same bug that I had."

From these words, Sarah knew that no information had leaked out about the happenings at the clubhouse the day before.

"Sarah, can I help you with anything?" Lillian inquired.

"No, I just came down to check on things for tomorrow and to type my agenda."

As soon as the words were out of her mouth, Sarah remembered the last time she had been typing on the computer at the clubhouse and what had followed. She was glad it was daytime, and that Lillian, Raymond, and Joe were all in the building.

It is going to take a long time before I will venture down here by myself again at night. In fact, maybe I never will, she thought to herself.

Sarah finished her work just before 11:00 a.m., and with still an hour left before she was to meet up with Detective Smith and feeling very restless, she decided to visit Penny Shriver at the hospital.

Once in the hospital, she immediately headed for Penny's room which was on the second floor in the south wing. Penny was sitting up in a chair, reading a book when she entered her room.

"Penny, how are you doing?" Sarah asked.

Penny jumped at the question because she was totally engrossed in what she was reading.

"Sarah, how nice of you to come. I am doing fine. The doctor is going to let me out tomorrow morning, and I plan to be at the luncheon tomorrow."

"I am glad to hear that."

Sarah and Penny then embarked upon a half-hour's worth of conversation. Sarah, in particular, filled Penny in on all that had taken place involving Ed Porter since Penny had been taken to the hospital. Needless to say, Penny was shocked.

Suddenly realizing it was fast approaching noon, Sarah said goodbye to Penny and headed to police headquarters. Detective Smith was anxiously awaiting her when she arrived.

"I am so curious. What information do you have to tell me?" Sarah asked.

"I have lots to tell you," Detective Smith answered. "But first, I want to know how Penny Shriver is doing?"

"I visited her before coming here. She appears to be doing very well and expects to be at the clubhouse for the luncheon tomorrow."

"That is certainly good news. And how are you doing?"

"I am fine. Still a bit shaken by all that has been happening but fine."

"I am happy to hear that. I think what you need is some closure, and I have information that might just provide that for you."

"Now you really have piqued my curiosity."

Detective Smith began. "After his arrest, Matt was taken into police custody and 'booked' or 'processed.' Sarah, do you know what happens during a booking?"

"No, I guess. Not really. I have never before known someone who was actually booked for a crime," said Sarah.

"Well, there is a real system involved in doing a booking. First, vital information is recorded, and mug shots are taken. The suspect's height and weight are put in the photos. After the mugshots, personal clothing and property are confiscated. In Matt's case, no contrabands such as a pocketknife or anything considered evidence was confiscated, but interestingly, he did have $1,000 in his wallet. When asked about it, he said it came from his latest gambling winnings."

"That is certainly interesting, considering he told us that he had just lost lots of money gambling."

"Matt seems to have trouble with reality," said Detective Smith and then continued. "Matt was then given his orange jail uniform, and his personal belongings were put into safekeeping until he is released. Next, he was fingerprinted, and these prints will be kept in a database indefinitely."

"Were Matt's fingerprints found at the clubhouse?" asked Sarah.

"Yes, his prints were found in the kitchen, the downstairs hallway, and in the rental office. They are being used as evidence against him."

"How about DNA evidence?"

"Matt was asked to deliver up saliva for his DNA sample, but it is unlikely that his DNA will be useful in proving his part in the murder of Ralph Benson."

Detective Smith then mentioned that Matt had to submit to a full-body search to make sure he had no weapons or other contraband on him which could be brought into the holding cell.

"I certainly hope they did not find any weapons or contrabands during Matt's body search," said Sarah.

"No, nothing was found, and a search through the database to make sure he did not have any outstanding warrants did not turn up anything either."

"I am glad to hear that."

Continuing, Detective Smith added, "Matt underwent a general health screening to make sure he was neither in need of immediate care nor a threat to officers or other suspects being held. He received a clean bill of health. Once booked, he was then placed in a holding cell. He is presently in the county jail until his arraignment.

"What will happen at the arraignment?" asked Sarah.

"During a typical arraignment, a person charged with a crime is called before a criminal court judge, who reads the criminal charge(s) against the person—now called the defendant—and asks the defendant if he has an attorney or needs the assistance of a court-appointed attorney. The judge then asks the defendant how he or she pleads to the criminal charges—guilty, not guilty, or no contest. The judge then decides whether to set bail, and in what amount, or to release the defendant on his or her own recognizance. Dates of future proceedings such as pretrial motions and trial are announced. Also, the prosecutor will give the defendant or his or her attorney copies of police reports and any other documents relevant to the case."

"When do you think the arraignment will occur?"

"Shortly after Matt is announced as the suspected killer of Ralph Benson."

"I guess this will be the first time Alex and Katie will see their father since his arrest. Are they going to be able to talk with him?"

"I will see if I can arrange a time for them to meet with their father either at the county jailhouse or at the courthouse before the arraignment. I hope I can arrange a courthouse deal. I think it will be less traumatic for Alex and Katie."

"I agree. Thank you for any help you can give them."

"I am happy to do whatever I can for them. They are such nice kids and have been dealt two terrible blows."

Detective Smith then revealed that he had even more information for Sarah.

"I saw Matt Lowe early this morning and he handed me a letter that he wrote to you. I know that this letter will help you understand what has happened."

Detective Smith handed the letter to Sarah, and she began reading.

> Dear Sarah,
>
> I feel that I need to explain some things to you. First, I want you to know that I have not always been a gambler. I became enticed by it when I went on a three-day business trip to Las Vegas two years ago. I had always wanted to find out what Las Vegas was all about and was excited to get my chance. During my free time there, I visited a couple of casinos and immediately thought, *Las Vegas is great!* I think I was immediately attracted to the glamour, the entertaining atmosphere of the mainstream gambling scene, and the high energy in the casinos. On that trip, I only tried the penny slots and left ahead by ten dollars.

When I came back from Las Vegas, I started to visit the casinos in Atlantic City. At first, I only went once a month and then gradually I moved on to making trips at least once a week. I found that once I walked into the casinos and heard all the bells and whistles and the clatter of coins spilling out of the machines, I immediately perked up.

I started with the penny slots and quickly went on to the quarter and dollar slots. Next, I began doing the high-limit slot machines which require relatively large bets in order to play. They attracted me because they have multiple advantages over low-limit slots. Higher-limit games offer a higher percentage payout and usually have their exclusive section in the casino where you can play. High rollers also are offered better perks than low rollers.

As time passed, I became bored with the slot machines and moved on to blackjack and other table games. I found it all great entertainment and an opportunity to win lots of money quickly. I also felt a sense of belonging there. The staff was friendly and so were other gamblers. There was a true sense of camaraderie.

Now, not only did I spend an increasing amount of time gambling, but I also started to bet large amounts, for example, hundreds of dollars per hand at blackjack. I was winning all the time. But then I began to lose, and I felt I needed to play more to win back the money I had lost. My gambling became a vicious circle. When I won, I wanted to win more, and when I lost, I wanted to win back what I had lost.

Regardless of whether I was winning or losing, I could not stop gambling. When I ran out of cash, I turned to my line of credit and then to my credit cards. Soon, all was maxed out. I was desperate to get more money. One of my gambling buddies put me in touch with a licensed loan shark who could lend me money. It seemed that it would be less hassle and more private than trying to get a loan from a bank. Little did I fully realize how costly and dangerous it would be to borrow from him. The loan shark started out being very friendly as long as I kept up my repayments. But as I borrowed more, money came at a higher price and when I did not pay on time, I was severely harassed.

I also want to tell you and emphasize that Peggy had no idea while all this was going on. She knew I was making a good salary and that we should have more than enough money to cover our expenses and to assist Frank and Janice. Peggy only learned about the horrors of my gambling addiction the night she died.

I also want to explain why Peggy and I were not at La Bonne Vie. I went to Atlantic City that morning and called Peggy about 4:00 p.m., telling her I had car problems—a lie—and that I would not be able to make it for the dinner. She said she did not want to go without me and that she would make up an excuse for us, which I guess she did. I never heard what happened.

After Peggy's funeral, I told Alex and Katie that I had to go on a business trip. But I am sure you can guess what I am going to say. Of course, I did not go on a business trip, I went to Atlantic City. I wanted to have a big win to overcome my despondency over Peggy's death. When I showed up at the clubhouse the other day, I was just returning from there after having lost $10,000. I was completely out of my mind.

I am so ashamed that my gambling addiction has ruined everything. I caused my children to lose their mother and Monica and Ed to lose their daughter. And I still cannot believe that I actually felt so desperate that I murdered Ralph Benson in cold blood. I am so, so sorry for my truly wicked behavior.

And Sarah, I apologize to you for having disrupted your life and for having caused so much havoc at the Women's Club. I hope one day, you will be able to forgive me.

Sincerely,
Matt

At this point, Sarah was in tears.

"It is so sad that gambling is so insidious. It presents the illusion of easy money, yet it can quickly lead to financial ruin and worse. The odds are never in your favor."

To give Sarah some positive news, Detective Smith said, "I checked out the story of the two guys who paid a visit to the Lowes' house last night. It seems that they are the strong arms for a two-bit loan shark with whom Matt Lowe has been doing business. I plan to pay the loan shark a visit today to let him know that Matt is in jail and that he is to back off from harassing the Lowe and Porter families unless he wants to end up in jail too. I will let you know the results of my visit to him."

By now, Sarah was completely overwhelmed by what she had learned. She thanked Detective Smith for all he had done to help her understand Matt Lowe's actions.

Detective Smith then continued, "We still need to fill Alex, Katie, and Monica and Ed in on Matt. I am going to contact Dr. Carrillo and find out if Ed is strong enough to handle the news. If he is, then I would like to speak to the family members in Ed's room at the hospital. Will you be available later this afternoon to lend support?"

"I can arrange my schedule however you want. In the meantime, I think I will go home and relax and try to digest all that you have told me."

"Sounds like a plan. I will be in touch soon."

"I will be awaiting your call."

CHAPTER 19

Answers

Sarah received a call from Detective Smith at 3:00 p.m. He told her that Dr. Carrillo was sure that Ed Porter was strong enough to hear the news about Matt. He had added, however, that if there was any problem, Ed was in the perfect place to receive medical attention right away.

"Since we have Dr. Carrillo's go-ahead, Sarah, can you meet me in Ed's room at three thirty?"

"No problem. I shall be there."

Before leaving for the hospital, Sarah called Bob to let him know what was happening and to see if he could possibly be at the hospital at 3:30 p.m.

"I am sorry, Sarah. I have a client meeting then, but I will come to the hospital as soon as I am free."

"I am glad you will be coming to the hospital. The Lowes and Porters will need your support, but I know I will need it too."

"Sarah, stay strong. I love you."

"I love you too."

Sarah hung up the phone and left for the hospital.

At three thirty on the dot, with Alex, Katie, Monica, Ed, and Sarah all assembled in room 205. Detective Smith, as gently as possible, filled them all in on Matt Lowe's recent activities. In particular, he detailed his gambling problems and how they had led him to murder Ralph Benson.

"How do you know that my father murdered Ralph Benson?" asked Alex.

"He admitted to it."

"When did he do that?"

"Two days ago, your father showed up at the Women's Club. He had heard that Raymond Garcia was going to be the new custodian at the club. He went to the club to confront Sarah and make her retract her offer to Mr. Garcia and to hire Frank Millard. He stormed into the club rental office where he found Sarah; Laurie Johnson, first VP; Penny Shriver, the rental manager; and Raymond Garcia. He told Sarah she had to hire Frank Millard or else he was going to kill all four of them. She tried to explain to him that Frank Millard was not getting the job at the club because he already had a job, but your father would not listen to her. Finally, she just agreed to call Mr. Millard and offer him the job. She made the call but ended up leaving a message for Mr. Millard to call her back."

"I don't understand. Why was it so important to my father that Frank Millard get the custodial job?" asked Alex.

"Good question. Sarah asked him exactly that. He told her that he had lots of gambling debts and owed a lot of money to dangerous people. And, because of that, he could not give any more money to Frank and Janice Millard. He needed Frank Millard to have a full-time job."

"Did my mother know all this?"

"No. not until the night she died. As I understand it, that night, your mother innocently asked if they could increase the amount they were lending to Frank and Janice. Your father lost his cool. He detailed for your mother what had been going on with him, and how he had tried to stack the deck at the Women's Club by killing Ralph Benson so Frank would get the custodial job. At first, your mother didn't believe him, but then he showed her his gun. She was very upset and ran out of the house with it and jumped into the car. It is presumed she was heading to your grandparents' house for help when she crashed."

"Wow, so my father did not tell us the full truth about why my mom had raced out of the house the night of her death," interrupted Katie.

"No, he did not. But let me continue with what happened at the Women's Club.

"Joe Finnegan, the retired policeman who had been doing custodial work at the club, called the rental office from the club kitchen, and Sarah used his call to pretend that she was speaking to Frank Millard and offering him the custodial job which he supposedly accepted. Your father appeared pleased with this, so after Sarah put down the phone, she asked him if everyone could now go. But he suddenly took an about-face and said that he had no choice but to still kill all of them. He fired a shot into the wall to show that he was serious."

"I can't believe my father acted this way. He has always been calm, cool, and collected. I have never seen him do anything hostile to anyone," said Katie, crying.

"How did you get away, Mrs. Peterson?" asked Alex.

"Thankfully, Joe Finnegan burst into the office and was able to stop your father from killing everyone, but not before his gun went off again and wounded Penny Shriver in the leg," responded Sarah.

"Is she okay?"

"Yes, she will be fine."

"What happened next?"

"Your father and Joe wrestled with each other for several minutes until suddenly your father got free and ran out of the room. Joe and Raymond ran after him across the balcony, down the backstairs, and they were heading to the kitchen when they caught up with your father who had been apprehended by Detective Smith. He was being handcuffed and read his Miranda rights. He has been booked for the murder of Ralph Benson and the attempted murders of Sarah Peterson, Laurie Johnson, Penny Shriver, and Raymond Garcia."

Alex, Katie, and the Porters sat in stony silence, reflecting on all they had just learned.

After a few minutes, Alex asked, "Where is my father now?"

"He is in the county jail. If you wish to see him, I can arrange it," Detective Smith said.

Alex did not say anything else, nor did Katie or Monica or Ed so Detective Smith continued, "I do have some good news for you. I paid a visit this morning to the loan shark who had sent those two thugs who harassed you last night. Some pressure was put on him, and you should have no further trouble from any of them. You may return to your home."

They all thanked Detective Smith for his continuing help. At this point, Captain Blanchard appeared and came into Ed's room. He asked if anyone had any questions, and when none came forth, he explained the awkward situation he was in. He said that he would like to keep the identity of Ralph Benson's killer under wraps a while longer, but that he had no choice but to reveal it. The media was exerting much pressure in order to learn who the murderer of Ralph Benson was, and he was afraid that someone on the inside track might release the information. He, therefore, was making the decision that during the five o'clock news that evening, the name of Matt Lowe would be released as the killer of Ralph Benson.

Everyone sat quietly at hearing this news, except for Katie who began to cry.

Captain Blanchard and Detective Smith then left for police headquarters to ready themselves for the 5:00 p.m. news briefing.

As 5:00 p.m. approached, Alex turned on the TV. The lead reporter for the evening news began, "We have breaking news this evening. I turn now to Captain Blanchard of the Calm Woods Cove Police Department."

Captain Blanchard surrounded by Detective Smith and 4 other officers spoke. "Good evening. The last time I spoke, I said that we had arrested a person of interest in the murder of Ralph Benson, but that we could not at that time release the suspect's name. Well, tonight I am able to do that. I am here to announce that Matthew 'Matt' Lowe, fifty-one, of Calm Woods Cove has been arrested for the murder of custodian Ralph Benson who was found shot to death in an office at the Calm Woods Cove Women's Club."

At this point, a photo of Matt was shown on screen, and then the cameras turned back to Captain Blanchard who continued, "Mr. Lowe is also being charged with the attempted murders of Penny Shriver, Sarah Peterson, Laurie Johnson, and Raymond Garcia at the Calm Woods Cove Women's Club. It was during the attempted murders that he revealed that he had murdered Ralph Benson with multiple gunshots to his head and body. He has been transported to and currently remains in the Vista County jail. Both incidents remain under investigation. Further information will be forthcoming in the days ahead."

While Captain Blanchard was speaking, Bob arrived in room 205, ready to give his support to all who needed it. He was surprised to see that everyone was extremely calm and quiet. In fact, they appeared to be in shock. Then suddenly, Ed Porter asked his wife to find Dr. Carrillo because he was feeling like he was going to pass out.

"I will go find Dr. Carrillo," offered Bob. "Monica, you just stay by your husband."

Bob left the room. After fifteen minutes he had not yet returned, and Ed was starting to look very weak.

"I certainly hope Dr. Carrillo is in the hospital," said Sarah.

Finally, a few minutes later, Bob and Dr. Carrillo entered the room. Dr. Carillo hurried to Ed Porter's bedside while at the same time asking everyone else to wait out in the hall for a few minutes while he examined his patient.

"Ed, tell me what you are feeling," said Dr. Carrillo. "Do you sense that you are experiencing arrhythmia?"

"No, physically, I think I am fine. I just cannot come to grips with the fact that my son-in-law has caused me to lose my only daughter. I don't think I will ever be able to forgive him. And, in addition, to think that he killed another human being all because he had gambling debts. I thought I knew Matt, but I certainly did not. He has turned out to be a very sick man. My poor grandkids have no mother thanks to him. He is a disgrace."

"Ed, I am so sorry for you, for Monica, and for Alex and Katie. I think one day you may be able to forgive Matt, but I am sure that day will be a long time coming. But right now, Monica, Alex, and

Katie need you to help them get through this awful situation. They need you to be strong."

"I know. You are right. But I am not sure I am up to being strong."

"I am sure you are. Think of your daughter and try to figure out what she would like you to do in support of her mother and her children."

"I will try."

"Please feel free to call on me for support."

"Thank you for listening to me."

"Now, unless there is something else I can do for you, I am going to call the others back into the room."

"No, there is nothing else you can do for me, except say some prayers that I can be strong for Monica, Alex, and Katie."

"I will be happy to do that."

Dr. Carrillo then called the others back into the room.

"I am happy to report that Ed is fine. He just needs rest and your support. I will look in on him tomorrow morning and most probably will discharge him from the hospital then."

Hearing this, Monica went over and gave her husband a big hug and kiss.

As soon as Dr. Carrillo left the room, Ed mentioned that he was getting hungry. He hoped his dinner would be arriving soon.

"Why don't I go get a pizza so we all can eat together?" Bob suggested.

"Great idea. I'll go with you," said Alex.

Fifteen minutes later, with two pizzas in hand, Bob and Alex returned to room 205. And as luck would have it, Ed had just received his hospital dinner. When he looked at it, he was sorry that he could not enjoy the pizza with the others.

During dinner, there was little conversation, and what there was centered on Ed's health. No one said one word about Matt and his arrest.

About 7:00 p.m., Bob and Sarah decided it was time for them to head home. As they were leaving, Sarah invited Ed, Monica, Alex, and Katie to join her table at the Women's Club's Annual Luncheon the next day. They all graciously accepted including Ed who added, "As long as Dr. Carrillo comes through and releases me."

"I hope all of you enjoy a good night's sleep tonight," said Bob.

"I hope so too," said Monica and then added, "We are so grateful, Bob and Sarah, for all your support." She then began to cry, and Sarah wrapped her up in a big hug. Hugs all around after that and then Sarah and Bob left the hospital.

Arriving home, Bella greeted them enthusiastically. It was a particularly beautiful evening, so Sarah and Bob decided to walk the neighborhood with Bella.

"Look at that sunset," said Bob. "It almost makes you forget that a close friend has just been arrested for murder and his two children have lost their mother because of his reckless behavior."

"It truly is a devastatingly sad situation," Sarah added.

Before the conversation got any more emotional, Bella started pulling on the leash and barking excitedly.

"Bella, what's the matter?" asked Bob.

As soon as the question was out of his mouth, Bob knew the answer. Around the corner came Bella's friend, Frenchie. His owner brought him over to see Bella. The two dogs were delighted to see each other. After a few minutes of fun together, the dogs were taken in opposite directions.

Bob, Sarah, and Bella continued their walk for another twenty minutes and then returned home. Sarah checked to make sure Bella had enough food and water in her bowls and then gave her a couple of treats.

"Looking at Bella enjoying her treats, I think I would like some dessert," said Bob.

Sarah offered him apple pie a la mode, which he gratefully accepted.

Bob and Sarah were enjoying their pie, when the phone rang. It was Amy.

She was quite concerned about Sarah after seeing the nightly news and learning about the arrest of Matt Lowe. Sarah assured her that she was fine but suggested that she give Alex and Katie a call and offer her support.

"I will be home soon for the summer, so I should be able to help them whether they are in Calm Woods Cove or in Connecticut," responded Amy.

"I will be seeing them tomorrow at the Women's Club luncheon, so I will tell them that you will be home this summer and would like to get together with them."

"Are Ryan and Elizabeth still visiting you this weekend?"

"Yes. Are you going to be able to come?"

"I wouldn't miss it."

After some further light conversation, Bob and Sarah bid their daughter goodnight.

As soon as they hung up the receiver, the phone rang again. It was Ryan who, after seeing the news report about Matt Lowe, was also checking to see how his parents were holding up. They assured him that they were fine and looking forward to meeting Elizabeth on the weekend.

Just as Bob and Sarah were getting ready to retire for the night, Michael called. He, too, was concerned about the effects of Matt Lowe's arrest on his parents and was particularly interested in what was happening to Matt in legal terms. At the end of his conversation with his parents, he affirmed that he would be coming for the weekend to meet Elizabeth.

"It is so nice that all three of our children will be with us this weekend. I know I need something happy to be occurring after all the negativity of the recent past," said Sarah.

Bob went over and wrapped Sarah in his arms. "I agree. It will be very nice to have all three home, and I am really looking forward to meeting Elizabeth."

"I am too. Perhaps, I will be one of those dreaded mothers-in-law in the not-too-distant future."

"Sarah, I know you well, and you could only be a wonderful mother-in-law."

"Thank you. I hope I can live up to that."

"Not to worry. I am sure you can."

"Well, I guess I better get some sleep so that I am up to the festivities at the Women's Club tomorrow. I am hoping all goes well at the luncheon so that we can end the club year on a positive note."

"Do you have any reason to think they will not?"

"No, I have just become a little pessimistic since so many awful things have happened at the club recently."

"But remember, they all had to do with Matt Lowe. There is no reason to think that awful things will continue to happen now that Matt is locked up."

"I know, but I will be glad when tomorrow is over, and I can concentrate on family doings."

"Speaking of family doings, do you have any special ideas of what we should do to entertain Elizabeth?"

"I have a feeling Ryan knows exactly what he would like to do when they come, starting with giving her a grand tour of Calm Woods Cove."

"You are right."

"I think we should give him a call Thursday night and find out what he is thinking."

"Good idea."

"Well, now it is definitely time for sleep."

Bob and Sarah prepared for bed and then fell asleep in each other's arms.

CHAPTER 20

Coming to a Close

Sarah awoke Wednesday feeling like a new lease on life was about to begin. She was actually smiling as she glanced out her kitchen window while preparing breakfast for Bob and herself. Bob entered the kitchen and caught her smile.

"It is so nice to see you smiling. Are you thinking about anything in particular?"

"I was just thinking that I feel it in my bones that today is going to be a particularly wonderful day."

"And why do you think that?"

"I'm not sure. But I hope my feelings are right. And also, look out by the garden."

Bob did as commanded and he, too, began to smile. There were five deer, two of which looked to be quite young, nibbling on leaves and flowers.

"No wonder you were smiling. Even though they are eating our leaves and flowers they are truly beautiful animals to behold."

Following the lead of the deer, Sarah and Bob turned to enjoying their own breakfast. They enjoyed scrambled eggs, juice, and coffee. Bob then left for work, but not before telling Sarah he hoped all would go well at the club's annual meeting.

Sarah tidied up the kitchen, took Bella for a walk, and then went to dress for the meeting and luncheon. She had put much thought into what she would wear and had finally decided on white linen slacks, a white crochet sweater shell, a sun-kissed coral linen jacket, and sepia ankle strap wedges. She completed her outfit with a pretty paisley scarf, pearl earrings, and colorful bangle bracelets.

I guess I am ready to meet the world, Sarah said to herself and then took one last look in the mirror to be sure. She then left for the clubhouse.

Sarah arrived at the clubhouse a full two hours before the start of the Annual Meeting and Luncheon. This was going to be Raymond's first really important event since being hired as custodian. She was glad Joe was still around to help him because she knew what critics some of the women could be, and she did not want Raymond to receive any negative feedback.

Sarah found the two men out in the garden area. The garden looked absolutely beautiful with two dark red azalea bushes, a magnificent magnolia tree, and several blue-and-white hydrangea bushes in bloom. There were also a large number of newly planted, multicolored New Guinea impatiens. The garden was truly alive with color. Since it was such a beautiful day, with only a few clouds in the sky and temperatures nearing seventy degrees, the women were going to be able to enjoy punch in the garden before going inside.

After giving overwhelming approval to the setup in the garden, Sarah went into the ballroom to check on things there. Sixteen round tables with eight chairs at each table filled the room. The tables were covered with light green tablecloths and white napkins. The centerpieces were multicolored cut tulips in frosted vases. The room looked stunning.

Sarah found the president's table and put place cards on it for her guests. She was going to be joined at her table by First VP Laurie Johnson, Captain Blanchard, Detective Smith, Alex and Katie Lowe, and Ed and Monica Porter. Sarah was so happy that Ed Porter was being released from the hospital just in time to attend the luncheon.

About eleven forty-five, the women started to arrive, and by noon, almost all the expected 120 women, dressed in pretty spring finery, were in attendance. While sipping punch, they engaged in lively conversation mostly having to do with the arrest of Matt Lowe.

It was unbelievable to them that a member's husband had turned out to be a cold-blooded murderer and had unintentionally caused his own wife's death—Poor Peggy! A majority of the members despised Matt for having killed Ralph Benson, a beloved employee, but at the same time, they felt sorry for him because of the ruin he had brought to himself and his family. There were a few, though, that had no sympathy for him whatsoever. All did agree on one thing—that gambling is an addiction not to be taken lightly.

At twelve thirty, the members were invited into the clubhouse ballroom to enjoy a festive lunch.

They were served a catered luncheon beginning with vichyssoise (a chilled leek and potato soup), followed by chicken salad with peas and water chestnuts, and an array of specialty breads, rolls, and breadsticks. Dessert was fresh strawberry shortcake. All the women seemed to highly enjoy their meals.

At 1:15, Sarah called the business meeting to order.

"Welcome to the Calm Woods Cove Women's Club's Ninetieth Annual Meeting. It is wonderful to see so many members here today."

She then called upon the members to stand for the Collect and Pledge of Allegiance which were led by Ruth Wilcox. Once all the members were seated again, Sarah said, "I am very pleased to introduce our guests of honor today. I think all of you know Captain David Blanchard and Detective Jack Smith."

Captain Blanchard stood up and walked to the podium and on behalf of Detective Smith and himself offered well wishes to the club members and promised to always help safeguard the club.

Sarah then called upon the Membership Chairman Carol Voigt to light a candle and read the names of members who had passed away during the club year and asked the members to rise and observe a moment of silent prayer in their memory. Four names were announced. The only name left was that of Peggy Lowe. Before her name was mentioned, Sarah asked Ed and Monica Porter and Alex and Katie to join her. Peggy's name was then announced, and at the mention of her name, many were heard crying. Peggy had been such a beloved member of the Women's Club. It was very hard for the members to accept her death. They were going to miss her very much. She had done so many wonderful things both for the club and for a number of them personally.

Sarah asked Alex to light the special candle the club had in Peggy's memory. He did so and then he thanked the club members for having been such wonderful friends to his mother.

Sarah hugged Ed and Monica Porter and Katie and Alex and told them that they were to be considered honorary members of the club and as such the club was open to giving them any moral or financial support they needed. They just had to ask.

This was received with heartfelt applause. Peggy's candle was blown out and given to Alex and Katie and then the Porters and Alex and Katie returned to their seats.

It was now time for Sarah to turn to the business of the day. She called out and thanked members who had just finished serving on the Board of Trustees and on various committees. She presented each with a small thank-you bouquet.

The last item of business was the swearing in of the duly elected trustees and committee chairmen for the upcoming club year. Each new trustee was presented with a red rose as a token of appreciation for their upcoming service to the Calm Woods Cove Women's Club. The new trustees received deserved applause from the luncheon attendees.

Sarah now began to wind down the meeting. She thanked the members who had put together the wonderful luncheon. She called Raymond Garcia and Joe Finnegan in from the kitchen. She wanted to make sure all the members knew that Raymond Garcia was the club's new custodian and that Joe Finnegan would be leaving the club within the week.

"Members, we owe much to both Raymond and Joe. Please, personally thank them when you get a chance. Also, please be welcoming to Raymond as he gets used to his new job."

She ended by saying, "Thank you, Raymond and Joe, for all the help you have given the club."

Before bringing the meeting to a close, Sarah said, "We have one last item to take care of—our fifty-fifty raffle. We have sold one hundred tickets at $50 each, so $2,500 will go to the club winner and $2,500 for the camperships for needy children."

Laurie Johnson pulled the winning ticket from a large bowl. The ticket read, "The Meals on Wheels Gang." The Meals on Wheels Gang were five club members who worked together to deliver meals to those in the community aged sixty or more who were homebound and unable to shop or cook for themselves. The five ladies screamed with excitement when they heard that they had won. Together, they made their way up to Sarah to receive their winnings. Once there, one designated member of the group announced that their $2,500 winnings were going to be donated to the nonprofit Community Meals, Inc. They were loudly cheered for their generosity.

The luncheon was indeed ending on a very positive note. Sarah wished everyone a good summer and exhorted them to rest up so that they would be ready to take on a new club year in September. She then gaveled the meeting to a close.

At the end of the meeting, Sarah truly felt that the cloud that had been over the Women's Club was now slowly disappearing. She was hopeful that the healing process would gradually take place over the summer and that when the club year began again in September, all would hopefully be back to normal.

As these thoughts crossed her mind, Captain Blanchard and Detective Smith approached her. They both thanked her profusely for the delicious lunch they had enjoyed. Captain Blanchard then took his leave while Detective Smith did not move. He then told Sarah that Matt was going to be arraigned the next day at 10:00 a.m. before Judge Leopold Miller at the county courthouse.

"Do Alex and Katie and the Porters know this?" asked Sarah.

"Yes, I just told them. I am going to meet them at the courthouse at 9:00 a.m. so that they will have some time to speak privately with Matt before the proceedings. I am hoping you can be present during the arraignment and afterward to give them support."

"I will definitely be there."

"I am glad to hear that. I am especially worried about Alex and Katie. At this point, I do not think they really believe that their father murdered Ralph Benson. I am not sure how they will react when Matt is charged with that crime."

"The death of their mother was very hard on them, but it was an accident. The fact that they may lose their father because of a crime he committed will be devastating for them. They have always been very close to Matt. And as far as I know, he has always been a very good father to them."

"I believe that is true too. That is why I set up this meeting for them before the arraignment. I am not sure, however, what will happen at it. I just hope it will provide an understanding of Matt's actions for his children and in-laws which will lead to a healing process."

"I hope so. Alex, Katie, and the Porters have been through so much. Do you expect Matt to plead guilty to his charges?"

"No, I suspect he is going to plead not guilty. He is going to say he suffered temporary insanity as a result of his gambling addiction."

"Do you think he will win with this defense?"

"No, I really don't. But we will just have to wait and see."

"Do you think he will be released on bail or on his own recognizance?"

"He is being charged with premeditated murder and attempted murder, and I don't see how a judge can release him either on his own recognizance or on bail. Just because he is in jail does not mean that he has gotten over his gambling addiction. Who knows what his gambling impulses might cause him to do if he is released?"

"It is a scary thought."

"Yes, who would have thought that gambling would have caused Matt Lowe, an upstanding member of the community, to commit first-degree murder."

Sarah added, "I am still having a very hard time coming to grips with Peggy's death for which he in my mind is responsible. I don't know how he can live with himself."

"The few times I have seen Matt since his arrest, he does not seem to show any contrition for what he has done. I think he believes he will be exonerated and back home soon," said Detective Smith.

"That is so sad to hear. I hope justice will be done, and Alex, Katie, and the Porters will be able to get past all the ugliness that has transpired."

"I hope so too. I also thank you and the Women's Club again for a wonderful afternoon. See you in court tomorrow."

"Yes, I will be there to help support Alex, Katie, and the Porters through what I imagine will be the most traumatic episode ever to happen in their lives."

ABOUT THE AUTHOR

A New Jersey native, Susan is a wife, mother of three, grandmother of nine, a poet, writer, photographer, and author of the new thriller Shattered Calm. Susan has an MAT degree in French and, for a number of years, taught high school French. Since retiring, Susan has devoted much of her time and efforts to writing and photography. Using her writing and photographic skills, she has created a line of notecards and greeting cards, "Novelty Foto Notes." She has produced flyers, posters, tickets, newsletters, and brochures for various nonprofit organizations in her town. Her photos, greeting cards, and short stories have won numerous awards on the local, state, and national levels.

Susan loves cooking and swimming and is an experienced volunteer. She enjoys working with and helping local organizations. One of these organizations is the inspiration for her book. She has been involved with activities at her local Woman's Club for many years. She served on its board in various capacities including as president twice and is well-versed in the intrigues of club life and the diverse personalities of club membership.

Susan is an avid reader, and most often, the book she is enjoying is a murder mystery. Her local Woman's Club has a wonderful old building as its clubhouse. The more often she was in the building, the more she realized it would be the perfect backdrop for a murder mystery. Coming to this realization, she ultimately decided, "Let the adventure begin."

CPSIA information can be obtained
at www.ICGtesting.com
Printed in the USA
JSHW011414240223
38181JS00002B/13